SOON COMES WALPURGIS

Soon Comes Walpurgis
A Collection of Macabre and Disturbing Tales

By
Robin Artisson

With
Elizabeth Driskell Ahmad, *Editor*
Larry Phillips, *Illustrator*

© 2016 Robin Artisson. All Rights Reserved. This book or parts thereof may not be reproduced in any form, stored in any retrieval system, or transmitted in any form by any means- electronic, mechanical, photocopy, recording, or otherwise- without prior written permission of the publisher, except as provided by United States of America copyright law. So there.

ISBN-13: 978-1540752413
ISBN-10: 1540752410

BLACK MALKIN PRESS
Concord, NH

www.robinartisson.com

To the Lady of the Marsh:
"I, the most
Adore thee present,
Or lament thee lost."

CONTAINED HEREIN

"Gwel-A-Throt" 1

"In the Court of the Pumpkin King" 15

"Jawbones" 25

"Lykeia" 30

"Marjorie" 40

"Soon Comes Walpurgis" 48

"The Account of Dr. Theophilus Pirard, Concerning the *Volkulak*, 1893" 58

"The Believers" 77

"The Daughter of Bel-Trabol" 110

"The Leering Well" 125

"The Man in the Mirror" 129

"The Witch Who Blighted Leekley" 136

"The Tale of Thorkell and the Troll" 147

"'Twas the Night Before" 184

"Meadowsweet's Red Chaplet" 194

*Thus do the generations of the earth
Go to the grave and issue from the womb,
Surviving still the imperishable change
That renovates the world; even as the leaves
Which the keen frost-wind of the waning year
Has scattered on the forest-soil and heaped
For many seasons there-
Though long they choke,
Loading with loathsome rottenness the land,
All germs of promise, yet when the tall trees
From which they fell, shorn of their lovely shapes,
Lie level with the earth to moulder there,
They fertilize the land they long deformed;
Till from the breathing lawn a forest springs
Of youth, integrity and loveliness,
Like that which gave it life, to spring and die.*

Percey Shelley, from Queen Mab

GWEL-A-THROT

*　*　*

I can't remember when I started walking the road to this place. If I think back too far, the memories turn into dreams which turn into nightmares- and then they turn into half-conscious mumblings and darkness. From that point, I wake up feeling hot with an aching head.

Every day, I walk down these lanes, constantly stopping to look at the endless miles of brambles that line the roads. They have blackberries in them; and I like to pick big, plump ones and smash them between my thumb and my pointing finger, watching the black blood flow into my palm. There are stains on my fingers and hands from it. I eat some of them, but often I find them to be bitter even when they looked ripe.

The sun never really shines here, but that is fine by me because She is never seen in broad daylight. It's only when the insects start to chirr, and the yellow moon peaks out from behind endless walls of jagged clouds that I start to feel stirred inside and alert. I feel purposeful again, looking across the dark landscape for the Lady who walked out of her grave to embrace me.

"They have blackberries in them, and I like to pick big, plump ones, and smash them between my thumb and my pointing finger, watching the black blood flow into my palm."

I don't eat much anymore, and I don't ever feel hungry. The thought of the Lady that I seek over-rides my sense of better judgment, any pang from my stomach and any need for comfort. There is no real comfort without her, and I will discover her again.

When I have to sleep, I do it curled up in the ragged blanket I carry on my back. I drink water from the bottle I carry which I fill from the streams that cut through this haunted, beautiful land. I walk these lanes; and when I think I hear a car coming, I step into the woods or lie in a ditch. Most of the time there is no car. I can't remember the last time I saw a person, and the last three houses I have seen were ruins of stone and wood with just chimneys still jutting upward.

Even though an ocean separates me from the Land where I was born, I still hear voices from that place out here on these lanes and moors. I can hear my mother fighting with my father, sometimes, in the distance. I think they might get closer, and sometimes I'd swear I can see them, but as always, they stop. He drinks; she leaves; it goes quiet out here.

I know that my Lady wants blood. Where she lives, there is only half a moon; and it is always dark. The people who live in the forests and villages of her land have cold blood and no body heat- they are all as pale as bones that have been picked clean by ants and dried in the wind. She took some of my blood; and even as I felt the terrible cold, I felt clear, blissful, at peace; I know she is leading me to where our love can finally be fulfilled.

This night, like so many others, a mist is rising. I am on the wet grass, moving quickly even though I feel more tired than I ever have. Under my feet, there is a long strand, a thread... I can see it, pale in the moonlight, laying on the Land, stretching into the distance. If I follow it long enough, I will arrive at her feet for this thread is wrapped around the long spindle She holds.

"... The last three houses I have seen were ruins of stone and wood, with just chimneys still jutting upward..."

I can see her face in the moon now- no- I can see that the moon has sent dozens of tears down to earth, and there they sit cold and white in the dark. It is a graveyard full of white stones, and here is where the thread leads. Some of the graves have been dug up, and the rotting wood of their coffins has been strewn about. The old church adjacent to the graveyard has a strange yellow glow coming from within- but I will stay out here with the trees and stones. I know She is nearby.

If I spill my warm blood on the ground here, She will come! She must! When her pale folk take warm blood, they become warm and remember many things that they had forgotten- I need to empty myself to be complete; they must fill themselves to do the same. It's a fair trade.

* * *

The cut wasn't hard to make, and it didn't hurt like I thought it would either. Blood looks very black outside at night, and it feels hot. Heat, life; here, my Pale Lady, come out of the Ground. Embrace me; kiss me; let me run my hands over your perfectly round breasts, smoother than silk; and let me taste your cold lips again.

I feel so weak now that I can only lie against a stone and look at the ground. I wonder if I'll die here... not that it matters. I can hear the sound of her approach already. A fox just barked and made a yelp in the distance, and I can feel the ground moving. There is a steady, light touch of feet on the ground- her feet; I know it. I can smell her.

I remember the first time I saw her, hiking these rural lanes. I remember how I felt lying in her arms and asking her name. She spoke without moving her lips, and She said I could never know Her name. I loved her all night and felt my heart pour out of me, an ocean of love pouring out of me, for this mysterious and cold woman who never stopped staring directly into my soul with her coal-black eyes. She drank blood straight from my chest, from my mouth, from my hands. I wanted her to swallow me whole, to never be parted from her.

"It is a graveyard, full of white stones, and here is where the thread leads..."

In the morning, I was alone, tired and freezing, face down in the woods near the great mound I had first seen her standing upon. I dreamed such madness- I saw the white dogs following her; the pale people who flitted along like bats; I saw the white strands of thread that cobwebbed the entire world- I saw what others cannot see: that we are warm, pulsing mortals stuck in an eternal web of white threads of death, and the ground beneath our feet that looks so firm and solid is just a crust that covers an eternal black void full of the regrets of the ages; and the forms of every dead thing. We are ripening, we humans, getting full and ripe, and then we fall below, severed from the vine of life that we are all unconsciously a part of. We go to join in the feast below the rotting hill.

There is no other point to our lives but surrender to the Great Dark that awaits. There was a time when I would have been frightened by such a prospect but not now. In that surrender, a strange wisdom arises- you find out who you are when you give up on being anything. And I am he who loves the Black-eyed beauty that rose from the mound, and who broke open the graves. I will join her at the feast below.

I saw that spectral feast, but the food was red dust. I saw dark rivers and great halls that resonated with a timeless splendor and a great macabre sadness. I saw a great black man, black as obsidian, with great spreading horns, sitting at the head of a table drinking from a cup of stone. I saw my love; the only love I will ever have; running through twilit fields and forests on a great white horse that had burning eyes. Oh, my angel, my goddess, my muse, my life, my soul, my hidden bride, my everything; please, deliver me from the torment of wanting you! I choose death and dust to be with you!

The next night after my meeting with her, I stayed near the hill. I slept on it. I didn't leave that hill for weeks. Finally, I had to start moving. People had come around, and I had run out of what supplies I had in my backpack. People had come one night, carrying lanterns and chanting something at the hill. I felt afraid; I didn't know what they were doing- but I knew they weren't her. It was a strange night; my dreams were chaotic so I moved on. I ran through darkness, and I didn't care if I ran head-first into something or tripped and bashed my head open on rocks. I didn't care about anything but Her.

I finally stopped moving, days later, and just cried. I slept day and night but a dreamless sleep. I woke up finally to see a woman in a brown jacket giving me a bottle of water and asking me my name. I couldn't tell her; I have no name. I am only the lover of the White Lady whose eyes were burned into my memory, and that memory had replaced all the others.

The woman who gave me the water seemed concerned, but I could tell she knew something. She was probably in her forties, I'd guess, but strong seeming with mousy brown hair sprinkled with grey. She told me something odd. She said "I see they are leading you. Act without thinking. And if there is something you need to know, just listen. Pay attention. It'll come to you."

I started to ask her a question, when she said "Shhh... you need to drink more water and eat something. You are not safe here, and you being here means that the local people aren't safe either. I can help you, but you must never mention me."

"I saw the white strands of thread that cobwebbed the entire world; I saw what others cannot see: that we are warm, pulsing mortals stuck in an eternal web of white threads of death..."

She put something in my pocket that looked like a piece of bark and said "Lay under an elder tree with this, and they can't see you. That way, they will say what you want to know."

I don't remember that woman leaving. I just hiked off that evening and down the endless lanes. Her advice was easy to follow- I was too tired and crazed to make clear thoughts, anyway. I just wandered over the nighted countryside and tripped and fell into a stream. I thrashed out and was dripping, freezing- and then I heard it.

I heard a haunting melody coming from downstream, and I walked down the banks as quietly as I could. Finally, I shed my backpack and kept walking with only my blanket.

I saw a blue light in the distance and saw at least nine people walking around in a circle around it. I couldn't see what was making the blue light, but I perched behind a tree and got a better look. There was a bad smell in the air, but I ignored it to peak around. I was shocked at what I saw, and I almost laughed out loud for now I knew that I was mad; I was certifiably out of touch with reality. There were no more consequences, no danger. I could laugh or scream or even run and grab one of these people and murder them with my bare hands- and nothing would come of it.

That's because I saw that these were not people- they had human bodies- and were naked, all of them, but they had the heads of animals. I couldn't tell what animals they were, but they all looked canine- like foxes or wolves or dogs. They weren't singing, but a beautiful song, sung in a woman's voice, floated everywhere. I didn't know how, but I knew it was Her, my one and only love.

I stood up and immediately fell down. The animal people were gone, but a woman was left with her back turned to me. She was waving this long pole around that had a huge bulb of thread near the top; it was a spindle or a distaff or something. She was singing to herself a song. This is what she said:

*"Never let the dark moon set, nor the sun be blind and hot
Never let an autumn leaf flutter to stone;
Never let the moon be full, nor the sun cruel,
That is the fondest wish of Gwel-a-throt."*

She got up and walked past me, and the blue fire faded. I looked at her, shocked- it *was* her. Every bit of me tried to lurch upward to grasp at her, but I couldn't move.

The next thing I remembered, it was morning; and I cried all day. By nightfall, I had started following the stream in the direction she had gone, and yelling at the top of my voice "GWEL-A-THROT!"

I was hoping it was her name. I knew it had to be. I had to be with her.

And right I was. I finally fell asleep next to an old road, and I woke up to see her standing over me. She was smiling, and I leaped up to embrace her. She bit into me again, and I felt a rush of great joy and peace as I felt her cold skin becoming warm. She looked at me; her lips now flushed red and dripping a bit and told me that I could make her do whatever I wanted because I knew her name. She only asked how I had discovered her name.

I told her I heard her sing it around the blue fire- and that she hadn't seen me though I lay under a tree near her. She seemed to realize what had happened- "under the stinking elder", she said- and she reached into my shirt pocket and plucked out the piece of bark. A dark look crossed her face when she saw it, and she asked who had given it to me. I told her quite honestly that I didn't know, and then she asked me to describe the person who had.

I started to give her the description when suddenly I stopped. I felt scared. Then I told her that I couldn't say- I was told not to, and that I was afraid I'd lose her again if I told. She smiled and said that she understood. She pushed me gently to the ground and made love to me again- but I realized, in my great bliss, that the sun was coming up; and when I felt her start to stand up, I seized her hand. I wanted to stop her from going.

To my shock, her hand was not a hand but a hoof- the hoof of a white horse. I looked at her in shock, but she was gone then- I only saw the leaves in the trees above me and the coming of the dawn.

I stood up and screamed "Gwel a Throt!"- and I was not disappointed, for even though I could not see her, I heard her whisper into my ear "follow my threads to the place where the dead go to lie... I will be with you there..."

Every night since then, I have seen the thread and seen her face in the mist. One night, I saw her running, naked, ahead of me- and when I caught up to her, she had killed a rabbit

"I finally fell asleep next to an old road, and I woke up to see her standing over me."

and devoured it raw- I remember the gore smeared on her face; and how her teeth were still so white even with the blood everywhere. I got tangled in thorns then, trying to follow her into the woods, and I lost her. But every night, I have seen the thread and followed it. It runs straight on, never veering off- it runs straight on into the great mystery. I know she spins it and waits for me at the other end.

I have finally come here, to the graveyard, to die in her arms. I know she is coming near me; I smell her now; I can almost feel her. I can feel the ground getting thin beneath me; I feel so numb. I can hear the pale people calling my name, and I know that a feast is prepared for me.

Gwel-a-throt, my Lady, will be there with me; we won't ever be apart. I think I can hear a horse breathing heavily... I feel so... distant now. I am one with the love that is stronger than death, and it lives here in the grave-ground... I spent my life running from death, afraid of the grave, only to live for the first time here among bones. Love and Life are found in the place you'd least expect... I'd share this with everyone, but I'll never see anyone ever again, at least not above ground.

***

IN THE COURT OF THE PUMPKIN KING

* * *

They have sent me on a journey, but they have not shown me the way; no map have I, no inkling of the landscape beyond the misty border. What I find in me is a voice of silence in the depths of me that urges me on, forever on. I came to a township full of men, women and their frightened children; and when I asked my way, all they could bring forth where crumbling maps, breaking to dust and ash with age. They knew not; I knew not; despite their protestations I had to go on.

Not knowing became my greatest strength; what had bedeviled me with doubt became my surest teacher as I moved through the shroud of indistinct mist and form. My teacher lectured and taught with leading questions, showed me glories and mayhems; the very best and utter worst that people and things could be and always left me yearning to hear and see more. I began to realize as I walked over field after field made quiet by wet and decaying leaves that I was more than a lost learner; I had another role to play in this strange world.

Somehow, the world needed this long walk through ruined streets, trackless forests, and sweet-rot scented fallow fields. Every now and again, the dark landscape would open, and I would see greenery and smell the scents of herbs, bread baking, and again see the sun. There arrayed in the midst of all this, was a house, as white as fresh snow, with people running and walking to and fro. Each family I met this way was happy to see me once they got over their wonder at my appearance; and when I left each, I took something away which I could never put to phrase.

I left something, too- no person would walk or run the same way again after my coming and leaving. I would always move on further into darkness, and soon I began to hear (as I had heard so often) the moans and pitiful cries of other people trudging in the waste. I seldom crossed their paths directly; but the few times I did, I saw their ruined bodies, pale skin, and sorrow-overflowing eyes. They wanted the green under the sun, but they had been turned out as I had been and sent wandering. They wanted what they couldn't have anymore.

I just stared at the first of these beings that I encountered somewhat frightened, but after a time, I began to try to console them by telling them to keep walking on- that they had a road like I did. Sometimes they stared at me with anger or confusion; other times, they just faded away. And I walked on.

Now, the time came when I knew that my journey was a prelude to a celebration. I didn't know why, but the dark land and the hoarse voices of crows in the distance began to seem delightful to me; even though the only towns or villages I came across now had been long abandoned and given over to vines and weeds, I could sense the former joy that had snaked around those walls and windows everywhere I went. Where had it gone? Where were all the people? They were sent on, like me, but at a much earlier time. The landscape itself was just that, I reasoned- a massive collection of corpses: the corpses of former lives.

They left their things to vanish back into the ground; their homes to become skeletons; and their own souls to fall into the deep and into shadow. But shadow was not my foe; in its cool and invigorating embrace nothing could chase me to my own hurt or harm ever again. To go on was freedom; to be able to find sun-break, green fields, ruined buildings, the face of a broken doll on the ground (once beloved by a young girl much like my own beloved girls) and to watch the moon fly on her great arc every night- it was the essence of poetry spread before me and inside me like the royal cloak of the Gods.

Now, I came into the land of the King of Pumpkins, his knotty and bulging orange head struck up high on a scaffolding of jagged thorn-wood. Around him, the gourd-people lit bonfires of bone- bones collected from ages of the world long past. As each bone burned, it sang a song- more of a groaning noise, I say- and imparted to the king the collected essence of that life, all its wisdom, joy, and sorrow. He became wise on his throne of thorn-wood, and his massive head split down the front, making the smile of all times and places.

"...Even though the only towns or villages I came across now had been long abandoned and given over to vines and weeds, I could sense the former joy that had snaked around those walls and windows..."

The gourd people were happy to see me; they were happy that I could see them. I joined them in many rounds of the drink they distilled out of mud and tears and listened to many of the bone-songs that the fires made. I heard the voices of men and women who had seen the world change and change again- I heard the voice of the man who first crushed grapes to make the wine that would ease the sadness of those who knew its mystery; I heard the voice of a woman who had collected the knotted umbilical cords of 300 children she had helped to deliver and wrapped them around a bough of wood- a bough full of life-magic for her ancient people who were all bones now.

I heard stories that no collection of mythology would ever recount, lost before the first book was ever dreamed of. I heard about how the sky had become a bull and fought a giant with a head of fire for the safety of the alder tree, and after he slew the monster, gave its fire to the tree for safekeeping. I heard about three stars that came to the earth and convinced the Indweller in the Ground to make the first human children- so that they could hear from above the music that only beings from the ground could make.

The misshapen gourd people were not alone with their grinning king and their muddy, tearful drink; among them strode smooth-limbed women that appeared to be human from the front but whose backs were hollow and full of the droning noise of bees and birds. These strange women were wantons, each and every one; they only wanted to love and be loved for as long as the fires of life burned. And those fires would never stop burning.

I ran over the King Pumpkin's fields until his fires became like a constellation in the distant darkness, and I went on. I went on, sure that no one had passed this way yet, but I could see faint tracks the told me others had. The only unexplored place, I began to realize, was my own wonder at the strange world. This sense of wonder was the only eternally new thing that existed, or ever would exist, and then something of the purpose of my long wandering became clear to me.

"Now, I came into the land of the King of Pumpkins, his knotty and bulging orange head struck up high on a scaffolding of jagged thorn-wood."

I figured that one day the gourd people would collect my bones and burn them for their king's pleasure. I only hoped for one thing- I hoped to the earth and sky that my sense of wonder would go on beyond my bones. And this blazing hope, this prayer before all powers, provoked a reaction from even further within me. One of the strange beings that I had long forgotten about, but who had been near me before my journey began appeared.

I thought that this entity was a man at first, but it seemed it had a beauty that only a woman's form could answer for. Then I realized that my visitor was not male or female, and it mattered not. A sudden wind stirred up and poured leaves all over my visitor, and then from the north, a cloud of rooks, all screaming in unison, covered him. When the commotion died down, all that was left was a young boy with a tranquil face who took my hand in his and walked on with me.

"Before you were, wonder was", he said. "It is amazing, profoundly so, and that is all. This wonder has no name; this amazement has no poem that can cope with its strength. It only has life to move through. As it goes, more and more go with it. The infinitude of which I speak is mother to Gods and men, blade of pains and sorrows, healing hand to the same. To this wonder alone belongs religion.

There is no end to the shapes it will assume; no end at all. Do not try to enumerate those shapes; you will fail. Succeed instead at celebrating each one that you encounter, and you will know the all. Be blessed to celebrate with all your kin the goodness of it."

And then, he was gone. I, too, went onward through the fields of Hallows.

***

"She gazed across the sea of dark hands, glaring, wild eyes, jawbones, and gaping mouths. She looked up; there, just a stone's throw from her, suspended in the Tartarean blackness, was Bloody-Hair."

JAWBONES

* * *

If the unquiet dead were not busy waving their jawbones about, they were doing something even more irritating: they were keeping them where they belonged and wailing about their poor, lost, and pitiful souls. Their complaints and howls didn't emerge as intelligible words; only groans and shrieks that sounded like rusty scaffolding collapsing from the side of a tall building.

Elspeth always felt the urge to roll her eyes when she was immersed in it; years of moving through the world of the dead had revealed to her a world not unlike the world of the breathing: a world of fragmented, confused minds wrapped in their own miseries, certain that the world was ending near to this time tomorrow, and convinced that each of them had a starring role to play in the drama of it all.

Death was clearly quite the letdown for them if this hellish din and frenzied waving of long-decayed body parts about was any indication. It was just more histrionics.

Elspeth knew that if she were a better person, she would feel sorry for them all. Their miserable and brief existences had been conjured up by the machinations of fiends, to work in a lather of sweat and tears, and die young for the increase of greedy landowners. The only thing put aside for these boors was a fireside story that made them feel important to the ruler of the universe himself. Their impoverished fantasies of gaining a kind word- or even a second of notice- from their powdery-faced mortal rulers easily transferred themselves to the foot of the throne of heaven.

A hand from one of the shades managed to get a grip on her lapel. Another of the dead tried to sink her teeth into the pale flesh behind her ankle. Though she was as insubstantial as the wind to the living, to the dead her undisrupted life-force made her seem warm and alive. The strange soul-stuff attracted like to like. Elspeth realized that they only believed they could touch her; what she was seeing and feeling were these wretched lemures begging her for help, projections of their own hearts.

Most of them were here in this Black Pit of Debts because they had jeered and laughed while others were tortured or murdered, or because they had aided the authorities in the capture and ruin of others whose bodies had been defiled for public spectacle.

"Never a leader nor a follower be," Elspeth thought. There are dark commitments and darker debts in either direction, and no White Christ to wash it all clean just like that.

She rose up, a comet sliding through velvet darkness, a moth luminous in the Underworld, and the dead below groaned louder. She gazed across the sea of dark hands, glaring, wild eyes, jawbones, and gaping mouths. She looked up; there, just a stone's throw from her, suspended in the Tartarean blackness, was Bloody-Hair.

Bloody-Hair never took her eyes off of Elspeth. When Elspeth had first learned to be like the dead, to leap away from her own paralyzed, cold body and fly in any shape she wanted, Bloody-Hair would have terrified her. Spirits that appeared to lack irises and pupils were just disconcerting. But she had grown accustomed to this, too. It was surely better than no eyes at all! Yes, so Bloody-Hair had big white splotchy eyeballs. So she hissed instead of speaking. So she dripped blood like a freshly killed deer hanging upside down on a hunter's beam and having its pluck pulled out. Compared to some of the things Elspeth had seen slumbering under Cragingalt, a blood-drenched woman with parts of her eyes missing was pleasant.

What Bloody-Hair's eyes couldn't see in life, they could see quite easily in death. "I will release you" Elspeth sent directly into Bloody-Hair's mind. "Point to him and I will release you."

Bloody-Hair gave her a look that might have frozen a small ocean. Her left arm shot out from her body, growing longer and longer, her left hand's forefinger pointing sharp like a razor spear tip. Elspeth followed the weird limb with her eyes and saw the remains of the man it indicated. How fortunate! He still had his jaw where it belonged. She knew she'd need to get him before he took to pulling it off.

Elspeth changed her shape- from woman to a deep black birdlike horror- and dove down, opening two jagged talons. She plucked her prey up from the midst of the dead. She flew straight up like an arrow until the sides of this infernal pit were no more and only the darkened peaks of great mountains spread out to infinity in every direction.

She alighted on a mountaintop. She tossed her prey onto the grey and stony ground as roughly as she could. The terrified shade struggled to crawl away from her, but she re-assumed her human shape and easily pinned him to the ground with her foot in his back. He squealed like a pig being pinned for slaughter. Elspeth put on her best growling menace- which was always hard for her because when she wasn't plumbing the depths of the Underworld and questioning the recently dead, she spent her days baking and sewing.

"I have lifted you up from perdition, Laird of Restalrig." Her voice was the cold itself. "I can cast you back into that pit just as easily. You deserve nothing less... but I could have the mercy to leave you up here if you will reveal to me this thing you know which can serve you naught in your present poor state."

* * *

A lonely bird was making a round, trilling call in the distance. The wind rushed heavy over the little house in intervals that seemed to be coming more and more frequent as the night wore on. Elspeth opened her eyes. Compared to the din of the dead, it was so very quiet. The wind was soothing. She forced her arms to move and rubbed her hands over her eyes and cheeks. Please, face, feel warm. Legs, feel warm. Move.

She got up. The head-rush came then the terrible, coppery taste in her mouth. She stumbled through the tattered cloth separating her sleeping-space from the smoky, grimy hearth-room and almost fell into the arms of the woman who got up to rush over and help her.

"Kirkyard at Lasswade." Elspeth forced herself to say. "One of the Mackenzie stones on the north side. That's where the old bastard buried it." Elspeth sipped from the wooden bowl of water that was offered her. She cleared her throat. "Don't forget to remind the good lady of what she promised us- else I could see her crawling next to her ruined shade of a husband a fortnight from now."

She finished the water which always tasted a little grainy to her and tossed the bowl onto a pile of wool next to her chair. Damned jawbones. What was it with the dead and jawbones?

***

LYKEIA

***

Once, a very long time ago, before there were any roads or farms, before there were any cities or even nations, there was a mother who had a little son and daughter that she loved more than anything in the world.

She lived with her two children with a small band of men and women on the side of an immense forest. They would hunt in the forest, fish in the river that ran through it, and live a happy life until the hardest winter the world had ever seen came upon them. The sky turned a deep grey, and thick clouds that never broke apart blanketed the world. The sun vanished; the coldest winds came, and with them, the deepest snow. The rivers froze solid.

Soon, the people were hungry, and then they began to disappear- to leave in groups of two or three to try and find a place where the sun still lived and where there was still food and water that wasn't frozen.

The mother who loved her children finally realized that if she didn't leave, she and her children would die right there by the snowy woods so she wrapped them as warmly as she could- which was not quite warm enough- tied snow shoes on herself and walked into the forest with them.

She was hoping to find wood, frozen berries, acorns, or perhaps a den of rabbits who were also trying to hide from the cold, anything at all- but she did not, and her hunger grew terrible. Her children wept from the hunger until they could weep no more. And these spirits of the wind and snow grew crueler- a blizzard came to finish the mother and her two children off for good.

In despair, not wanting her children to perish, the mother prayed to the spirits of the forest for help. She begged them to save her children, and she would give them anything in exchange for this favor. Though the frozen spirits of the trees remained silent, one spirit in the forest heard and answered: the spirit of the great wolf. It told the mother that if she would sacrifice herself, it would see that her children were spared from the hunger and cold.

Without thinking, the mother kissed her two sleeping children and agreed- and by the magic of the wolf-being, she became a great tree there at the center of the forest. And while her little boy and little girl slept, they became wolf-cubs happily bundled in new and warm fur and able to trot through the snow and sniff out mice below the snow and catch them. The wolf-spirit saw to it that they survived the terrible winter.

* * *

Many thousands of years passed, and then one day when the land was crisscrossed by roads, and farms with their orchards and fields and pastures full of cows dotted the land; there was one farm that was home to a happy family- a farmer and his wife who had a son named Tom and a daughter named Jeannie.

"And while her little boy and little girl slept, they became wolf-cubs, happily bundled in new and warm fur…"

Jeannie was a very bright girl who learned everything she could. Her mother made medicine and remedies from the plants and herbs of the nearby forest and treated all the people of the nearby village. Jeannie helped her mother find the herbs and prepare the healing mixtures. Jeannie also helped her brother and father milk their cow and collect apples from their small orchard.

One day, when Jeannie was alone picking apples in the late afternoon, she felt very strange. She had been having troubled sleep recently and waking in the night suddenly with strange dreams; but now she felt even stranger- and before she realized what was happening- it felt as though she were being overcome by a great fever. She dropped to the ground, and became a wolf.

Full of the energy of her new shape, she bounded away full of joy. She ran faster than she ever imagined deep into the forest, dodging stumps and leaping fallen trees, and hearing and smelling hidden things as vibrantly as only a wolf can.

She fell asleep in a deep reverie later that evening curled up as a wolf under an old oak and had a very special dream: She dreamed that another wolf came to her; a wolf that was really a little girl. The little girl-wolf revealed to her that she was her many-times great grandmother. She said that once, out of love, her own mother had sacrificed herself to save her, and that salvation had come to her by the gaining of a wolf shape.

She warned Jeannie to never tell anyone about her heritage or its legacy- She called Jeannie her beloved granddaughter and said that men and women who could not change their shape would fear her and hurt her if they knew what she could do.

Jeannie went home that night, after changing herself back into a girl, and told her worried parents that she had simply become lost. They prayed thankfully that their daughter came back, and no more was said about it.

* * *

Jeannie's life was very exciting after this curious turn of events. She always volunteered to go to the pasture to tend to the cow or to the apple trees on the side of the forest so that she could turn into a wolf and run through the trees, feeling the great power and freedom of it. But one day, things did not go so well for her.

On that day, she was walking to find her family's cow, when she saw two men sneaking into their pasture, from its far northern edge. She knew they were bad men, for they had an ill appearance, and she guessed that they had come to steal their cow, which was beyond value for her family. One of the men had a gun, the other a rope- and they began to tie their rope around the cow's neck.

Without another thought, Jeannie turned into a wolf and charged at the men, barking and snapping savagely. The armed man aimed and shot at the angry wolf, but the bullet only grazed its forepaw.

"One day, when Jeannie was alone picking apples in the late afternoon, she felt very strange."

Jeannie clamped her jaws around his arm and bit deeply. He screamed, dropped his gun, and when she released him, he ran like his partner, in great fear of the beast.

When Jeannie took the shape of a little girl again, her arm was bleeding from an angry wound. She returned home and said that she had cut herself on a sharp stone in the creek. But the men she had chased away told everyone that they were attacked by a wolf near the pasture of Jeannie's father, which alarmed everyone in the village.

But the story of how they wounded the beast on its forearm aroused the suspicions of Jeannie's neighbors, who knew that she was wounded on the same day, in the same place.

It was believed that people who could change their shape would retain any injuries they received in their animal form, while in their human form- so rumors began to circulate that Jeannie was a witch or a werewolf.

* * *

Before long, fear got the better of the people, and they decided to arrest Jeannie, but before they could, her mother gave her a bundle of bread and cheese and told her to leave, to take to the forest and hide, to spare her the hysteria of the local people. Jeannie left, but once she was in the forest, she tossed away the food and became a wolf and ran deep into the forest's heart, where no man would go.

Asleep there, a night later, she had another dream. Again, the little girl wolf came to her and told her that nearby was a small cave that went deep into the ground, and that Jeannie should go there. The next morning, in her human shape, Jeannie did just that, and found the cave, which led to a tunnel, a tunnel that slanted down and passed deep into the earth.

The tunnel kept going down, and Jeannie kept following it for a very long time, until it opened up into a world that was below this one. In that world, which was draped in a perpetual twilight, was a never-ending forest of deep green that echoed with the whispers of human voices, birdsong, and the distant howls of wolves.

Jeannie walked about the timeless forest until she came to a tree at its center- a massive tree, bigger than the others. And from inside the tree, came a lady, who told Jeannie that she was the Great Grandmother of all werewolves. She revealed how she had, out of love, given her own soul to the forest, so that her children could be spared, and how they became as wolves to escape the cold spirits of death.

She told Jeannie that she loved her, too, as one of her descendants, and told her, from that day forth, to call herself by her true name, which was Lykeia. She promised her that if she slept one night here, in the Forest Below the World, that she could return to the human world and be safe forever.

So Lykeia did, and when she woke, and returned to the World Above, she discovered that a hundred years had passed, though it had only seemed like a single night to her. Her parents, her brother, their farm, their cow, the village- all of it was gone. No one lived who remembered her, and she was alone in the vast forest.

* * *

"Jeannie walked about the timeless forest until she came to a tree at its center- a massive tree, bigger than the others. And from inside the tree, came a lady, who told Jeannie that she was the Great Grandmother of all werewolves."

So she stayed and lived in that forest the rest of her days, preparing herbal cures and remedies for the people who came to visit her. She was hailed as the greatest of healers, and people paid her good company, when they visited.

No one ever asked from what people she sprang, and she never said- but she spoke to the trees, and to the wolves and foxes, and to the birds, as though they were people, too. One day, while walking through the forest in her wolf shape, she met another wolf, and some months later, she had children of her own.

Those children, and their children, they long outlived Lykeia, who died peacefully one winter night many years later. No one ever saw Lykeia's offspring, but the old folk knew that her sons and daughters had most likely become wolves in the wild. In thanks to Old Lady Lykeia's many services to them, in gratitude for the many times her herbal remedies had spared their own children from fevers and illness, they pledged never to hunt or kill a wolf in that forest.

***

MARJORIE

***

MARJORIE ADKINS had said her prayers before bed every night of her life since she had gained the power of speech. Her diligence was a soul-deep art; the words flowed from her without effort. Each word was a wish for her God; each crossing of her body a rose for the Queen of Heaven. Pale and thin, given to illness easily, her growth to adulthood was perilous. But each of her days and nights in bed, shaking under the heat of fever or the chill of cold, was raised up to heaven, alongside her prayers.

Marjorie was not precocious; she was not daring nor willful. She sat alongside her mother, learned needlepoint, practiced her French lessons, and read her Bible- this was her earthly paradise. Things were soft; things were warm; things were quiet. Men struggled in the sleet outside; they crossed forbidding country on horseback or in coaches; they lay in blood and mud in far-away wars whose terrors were unknown to her and that was best. Her dutiful father came, and he went. And his labors in a distant firm in London kept the sprawling old manor-house above and around Marjorie, her shelter from the dark world.

Days came, days went, and seasons passed- and Marjorie was nearly a woman. She wrote meticulously neat letters to her friends and family, and in time, letters came back- always warm, always sweet. She called out to her mother or the chamber maids from her illnesses, and they came to her bedside. Once, she whistled to a bird from the east garden, and she swore that it called back to her as though it had really understood her. The way it looked at her; it didn't seem afraid of her... in a world of perfectly recited prayers and perfectly written letters, it was the most remarkable thing that had ever happened to her.

The day Marjorie's mother died was like any other day- prayers said, letters written, guests received, tea poured, things neatly arranged. Marjorie saw her lying there at the bottom of the stairs; her face and head turned at an angle that was unnatural; but her eyes strangely full of peace. Marjorie prayed, prayed again, and remained in prayer for the better part of a month. She prayed as her mother was put to rest in a cemetery of towering marble obelisks and stones, but it all seemed like a dream to Marjorie.

Marjorie's aunt came to live with her, and after a few weeks, it was as though nothing had changed. Her mother's sister was nearly identical to her mother not just in appearance but in behavior. She sounded like her mother; she walked like her. Sitting on the couches in the parlor, reading in the afternoon, Marjorie would glance from the corner of her eye and see her mother.

Another fever came and went- but this one was particularly bad. At several points, there was some doubt on whether or not Marjorie would survive. But she did; she felt like she was a ghost, but eventually the breath of life came back to her weak limbs and she could get up and walk about- return to the routine of things. She could appreciate the colors of the trees outside her window. She could love the sound of birds again.

She had prayed throughout her fever even in the depths of her delirium. It was like prayer was the only thing that she could do when all else was taken from her. But upon regaining herself, she realized something. There was a stone deep in her heart, a weight, a disappointment she could not shake. For years she had prayed as regularly as the clock ticking in the upstairs hall and never had she felt a thing in return. She sent countless letters made from the stuff of her own soul to heaven, but heaven did not respond. A simple whistle brought the lark to her that day, but years of devotion yielded nothing at all. Her mother's reward for an identical devotion was a distant husband and a broken neck.

For years she had felt these doubts, and for years, she had feared her own thoughts of this nature- but now something had changed. The interior censor that had made these thoughts impossible before was gone, and they tumbled freely about her head; impious devils making plunder of her security. She was good, wasn't she? A quiet life of prayer, never an opportunity to sin beyond some secret swellings of youthful pride, or concupiscent tendencies towards laziness? If that wasn't good, what was good?

"Marjorie saw her lying there at the bottom of the stairs, her face and head turned at an angle that was unnatural, but her eyes strangely full of peace."

These thoughts would not leave her, and her attempts to make them stop only made them seem louder and more insistent. If God would make a single answer to a single prayer- just fill her heart with the overwhelming feelings of love she always longed for, or give her one dream, or one simple intimation that he was there- she knew that she could be whole again. One dream of her mother stroking her hair telling her about how beautiful heaven was... anything would suffice.

Days came and went. Weeks passed. Winter came. No response. Just empty prayers in an empty house and fitful, featureless sleep. Life became white and grey, and heaven was vast and silent. Marjorie stopped eating. Her skin finally became as white as the snow outside, and the doctors that came to see to her could give her nothing to restore her appetite.

Prayer was her only power. God now had a choice to make; he could lift a finger- with effortless ease for one so mighty- and give her a single feeling; a single precious brush against her fading heart that she might know life still had some meaning, or she could die. And who wouldn't rather be dead than to live in a meaningless world?

And so it came to pass- on weak and trembling knees Marjorie prayed, deep in the night, when she should have been asleep. She had gone beyond pain or concern for life. Now, her mind and body together had become an open channel for heaven to pour some of its light downward- if heaven were real, or if heaven was so inclined. And it was in the deep and despairing silence of just such a night when Marjorie got her answer.

It started as a painful pressure on the back of her neck which made her spine feel like it was burning. Then it went away- but the surprise of it was enough to shock all of her senses back to aware. From deep inside her, the feeling began to emerge. It was in the dark corners of her room, too. It wasn't God; it couldn't be. It was something else, something dangerous. It felt like a large animal was lurking outside her door- the cracks, the distant sounds- footsteps? Had someone broken into the house? Had she died? Was it her mother's ghost come to take her away? Her mind filled up rapidly with ghoulish imaginings.

But it wasn't just her mind. The room was filling up with something that was pushing into her flesh. Her chest began to throb around her heart. A cold sensation filled her face, and with it came a calm. She had a moment of terrifying clarity: she knew she was in the presence of the tempter, the enemy of humanity, the old serpent who forever deceives the world. She had always known he was there, but prayer kept him far from the treasure-house of her heart. Now, there were no locks on that door. Now, doubt had opened the gates of her body and soul, and the wild animals in the woods outside were padding their way in. And with those wild beasts, came their king.

His voice wasn't raspy or terrible as Marjorie had imagined in her darkest moments- how soft it was, though deep and hard to understand. She strained to hear, and his voice came again- now she understood him better. He spoke directly to her- not to her ears, or her face, or her mind, but to her. She waited for the onrush of damnation, but it didn't come. His questions were strange, not what she expected such a being to ask, but she wanted to be asked; she wanted to keep talking to him.

The feeling of someone standing right behind her was overwhelming. Slowly, she looked over her shoulder. There was nothing there but the great mirror- which captured the whole scene: the back of her head, the back of her nightgown, her legs bent as she prayed on her knees. She looked at the mirror, but for the first time, the girl in the mirror wasn't looking back at her.

"Slowly, she looked over her shoulder. There was nothing there but the great mirror..."

She looked straight ahead. The room boiled; it was swimming with tangible forces, and they moved into and out of her flesh leaving a tingling feeling in their wake. He was behind her again. The house suddenly seemed very small, and the world seemed very large. Marjorie had gone beyond all pain. She knew she wasn't going to die; her prayers had, after all, been answered though in a rather unexpected way. And at the moment of death what dying person really cared who answered?

A lifetime of unanswered letters, and finally, a return letter is slid under the door by an unseen hand- who could fail to open it, and read every word with great curiosity and greater joy? She caught herself smiling- smiling for the first time in months.

Marjorie turned her head to the side and whispered softly to His presence behind her.

"You'll do."

* * *

SOON COMES WALPURGIS

***

Hope did not walk hand-in-hand with those poor souls who passed through the doors of Southwick Asylum. Their lot was a nightmarish parade of endless days: a cloudy dullness of the brain brought on by daily injections and bitter tonics, the dimness of half-lit halls, and musty grey sheets stretched taut across hard beds. The only thing crueler than the emotionless orderlies and magnanimous doctors who daily prodded the condemned of the asylum was the occasional hint of sunlight that shone through the narrow, peaked windows high on the wall of the hydrotherapy chamber: a reminder of the warmth and freedom that lurked just outside of this prison of faded green stone.

Ruth was only twelve years old when she walked through those doors. The drive down Bennet's Lane which overlooked the farms and orchards that rolled alongside the Miskatonic River would have been a pleasant one except that she was paralyzed by the fear and grief of her destination. She was helpless but not oblivious to the monstrous injustice that had been visited upon her. Nor was she unaware of the means by which her silence was going to be made final. Her step-mother sat smirking in the front seat of the Touring as it rattled through the cast iron gates of Southwick, cutting through the early morning fog. Her sour-faced father never spoke nor glanced at her once.

Locked away in the dark some weeks later, hearing only the distant cries and cackles of the patients sealed in the criminally insane ward below, Ruth turned to her only worldly possession which embodied all of her memories of the only person who ever loved her: the oddly-shaped doll with the dark porcelain head that her mother had given her which had originally belonged to her grandmother. It was all she had left of her mother who had died three years before of a sickness no doctor could understand or halt.

The paint of the doll's staring eyes had almost completely chipped off, and its hair had mostly fallen out; but as Ruth hugged it to her chest, shivering under the scratchy woolen blanket, she felt strange bumps on the doll's head- markings once concealed by purple silken hair. They were curious symbols that were barely seen by the dim light from the hall that fell across her bed. She sat up and strained to peer closer, but the doll was lost to her hands in the dark, tumbling to the floor and shattering into countless pieces.

Her knees were shaky on the cold floor, but Ruth didn't have time to weep for long- a strange visitor was waiting amid the shards: it appeared to be a brittle and yellow roll of papers, a strangely thick scroll, sealed by old wax. Also, amid the shards was a piece of dark amber which encased the strangest insect Ruth had ever seen. It was like no creature she had ever seen in a book nor while strolling in the woods or fields around her former country residence.

"The paint of the doll's staring eyes had almost completely chipped off, and its hair had mostly fallen out..."

The weeks that followed were less painful for Ruth even as the white-draped doctors spoke over her every few days and laid down plans to engage her in a "decisive treatment" for her "condition"- a procedure that would leave her a half-blind, emotionally-dead permanent resident of Southwick. At night when the heavy lock of her door thrust home, she read the fragile scrolls by the flickering hall-light as it fell through her small, barred window- scrolls written in the meticulous handwriting of a great grandmother she never knew. She pushed them into a small hole below her mattress when she was not engrossed in them, and every night she scrabbled to get them again. She read, and read more, and learned of things- dreadful things, wonderful things which defied all belief and which began to invade her fitful sleep.

Her family was more than it had appeared. To believe her great-grandmother, the women of her family were bound to a great and secret covenant which none outside their immediate circle of kinship must know of for the men of this world (so said her ancestress) would spill their blood with great fear and anger should the truth ever be brought to light. And the truth was itself beyond credulity: Ruth carried within her veins the same legacy her mother and all her grandmothers had carried: within her slept something that the laws of ordinary physics and the circular body of the natural elements had never given birth to. She was the many-times great granddaughter of a Father whose greatness far exceeded the visible boundaries of the horizon of this world.

The Ancient Father whose face could not be gazed upon by mortal eyes, and whose 366 savage and nigh-unpronounceable names her great-grandmother had lovingly recorded backwards (lest they be accidentally said aloud by a careless reader) still lived; for that Great Grandfather's complex organism of tangible and intangible fifth-dimensional matter could never be lastingly disrupted by simple tissue death. What part of his entity extended into the space of perceptible matter was coiled in his sacred dwelling place, wherein he brooded in a perpetual and ageless meditation far below the wide ocean that crashed upon the shore of Massachusetts.

Ruth learned that the whispering of only three of his names in a proper sequence and when the moon was waxing would allow her to transcend the limits of her bodily organs of hearing and grasp sound with preternatural clarity. She could capture the moans and rasping of patients all over the asylum as though she stood in the same room with them and as though she was bending forward to hover an ear inches from their foamy mouths. She could hear the dull conversations of the orderlies in the distant common room as though they stood over her and hear the birds outside as though they perched on her finger.

Another verbalization of the potent sounds- a certain sequence of thirteen of the names; all best whispered on the nights of the full moon (though efficacious on other nights)- gave her the power to leave her thin, emaciated body behind and run as a ghostly, unseen fugitive through the walls of the asylum and into the nighted forests beyond.

She visited her old estate-home, danced unseen and unheard upon the gabled roof above the room she had been born in, and soared like an owl amid the meadows and trails of the parks her mother used to take her to. She always returned with great bitterness to her tangible reality of bodily imprisonment and the glare of lights in the hallways of the asylum.

The creature in the amber was a mystery finally awakened by her on the hundredth day of her imprisonment using a chant her great-grandmother had revealed. The creature's astral guise was infinitely grander than the strange and puny insectoid body encased in amber which was all that the watery eyes of human beings could see: the creature came forth invisibly, and guided her, when she was free of her body, through the star-filled sky on its diaphanous and mostly transparent wings. Its many eyes were luminescent, and they shimmered with an ageless and malignant intelligence. The creature dutifully obeyed her every whim, sleeping in the amber when the sun was above head.

In the space of only four moons, Ruth learned that the astral wraith she assumed in her nocturnal outings did not prevent her from using the space-bending and heart-chilling sounds of her Great Grandfather's name to conclude other outcomes. With only an unseen stroke of her invisible hand across the foreheads of sleeping folk, and an astral whisper uncaptured by fleshy ears, she could thrust brain-rending visions of the terrors of the True Depths into their heedless minds.

Within the space of two months, her stepmother was dead of an overdose of Laudanum which she had gulped down in the acute delirium inspired by her refusal to sleep for weeks on end. The horrors she shrieked about nightly, before her untimely death, were all heard by Ruth's invisible ears; they were a song of justice sweeter than Dyer Street honey- and her stepmother's half-successful attempts to claw out her own eyes, rather than close them again in sleep, had added a delightful crimson ribbon to enclose this final gift of vengeance.

"...The creature came forth invisibly and guided her, when she was free of her body, through the star-filled sky on its diaphanous and mostly transparent wings..."

The orderlies at the asylum who had tormented her by soiling her food with filth began to miss their working days, and soon, were never seen walking the corridors again. One even became a patient of Southwick, diagnosed with extreme delusions and hysteria and suicidal ambition, and he sobbed and shouted long into many nights from beneath his saliva-soaked restrains, a sweet lullaby for Ruth.

But Ruth knew that her situation at the Asylum was growing desperate, as she knew from remotely hearing the reports and conversations of the doctors: within a fortnight, she would be reduced to a drooling waif and filed away in the basement as her frontal lobes were to be punctured and incised by the orbitoclasts of the surgeons. She was not brought here a murderess; she had not killed her beloved younger brother; it was her stepmother that had choked the life out of him. Yet she would be buried here for it, a living corpse with no future and no dreams.

Ruth knew she had changed; something had begun to awaken in her mind and her blood, and in her bones. She now had very little need for food though she was thirsty quite often. Chanting her Grandfather's names made strange visions swim in her sleep, and it summoned forth thoughts in her head that were clearly not her own. Though she was not yet thirteen years on this earth, she began to receive the memories and lores of someone many times older- someone who had at their command the unthinkable memories of ages.

She could not free her body from this hellish imprisonment, but she knew of one being that could- her Great Ancestor, whose ancient meditation she had disturbed with the chanting of his names. She had aroused him only an infinitesimal amount each time she spoke the forbidden sounds and borrowed from him only a fraction of his power to command the oneiric landscape of the unconscious soul, and yet, he was dimly aware of her, and she of his unutterable majesty. She longed to be with him in the deep.

Before all was lost, Ruth had decided- against her great grandmother's repeated written warnings- to ensure that the wickedness of the institution that now held her bound would not engulf her unto oblivion. She would do what was Never To Be Done, for she had to live, to teach her own daughters to come of their true heritage.

She had to make certain that the precious scrolls and the servitor slumbering in the amber never fell into the hands of the upright-plodding apes that called themselves "men", but whose weak, terrestrial blood and hominid genes bound them to doltish limitations in how they could think or dream. She had to make certain when the time was right- however distant the time might be- that her chosen line of descent would issue forth daughters, most favored, who would raise their hands in supplication and greeting when The Great Father returned to establish his kingdom on earth again.

Ruth knew that on Walpurgis Night- now only three nights hence- she could intone the litany of the 366 Names, nine times over with the tongue of flesh and blood, and then nine times in reverse with the tongue of the wraith, and awaken her Great Grandfather. She had studied; she had dreamed the sounds; she could say the names properly.

He would rise up; He would part the waves; He would smash asunder the hills and trees and the feeble dwelling places of men and come for her- leaving this hateful asylum a destroyed ruin all around her- just as He had brought ruin to great and proud Mantapor on the cliffs overlooking the Cerenarian Sea some twenty millennia before human beings had ever built their first cities. He would crush this cursed place as He had crushed the golden fleets of Rinar, leaving their shattered prows and scraps of their crimson sails to wash up upon the shore in distant Zakarion.

Ruth slept peacefully, waiting for Walpurgis to come, dreaming of the endless oceans, and of the secret greatness they concealed- and hearing, in the distance, songs sung in languages not born of this human earth.

***

THE ACCOUNT OF
DR. THEOPHILUS PIRARD,
CONCERNING THE *VOLKULAK*, 1893

* * *

Peradventure it will come to pass that an unprejudiced person shall read the account I make here; an account of the true history of the curse which came to haunt the distant Ciuluc hills in the troubled year of our Lord 1893; of the manner in which that curse consumed the lives of Christian men and women, destroying their purest and most innocent, and of the divine providence that established me capable of bringing this terror to an end, consigning it to the awful hell which was its origin.

I write this account for one who can speak no longer- a memorial and eulogy of truth to sweet Mariya Mozgovoy, whose life I could not save, though by my righteous vengeance her tormentor and murderer troubles this world no longer. I further write this account so that posterity will be schooled in the strange science which brings this curse to ceasing should it break loose once again.

I, Theophilus Pirard, native to Brugge, have spent the greater part of my life and career as an alienist studying and researching strange and exotic superstitions and the allied supernaturalism of primitive peoples. I have fathomed the secret doctrines of spirit-worship discernible in the mythologies of Europe and abroad and in the rude dances and chants of foreign peoples still untouched by civilization's light. In Europe, the eastern peoples of Roumania, Bessarabia, and the Bulgarian hinterlands still maintain something of their dark past of spiritism as do the Hindoos yet further east.

I had taken it upon myself to travel in these lands and collected many volumes of lore and accounts of preternatural phenomenon; some witnessed only briefly by myself but the larger bulk second and third-hand accounts of others. Before my recent sojourn into Bessarabia's dense forests, and the curious sequence of events which brought me into the house of the distressed Mozgovoy family and further into soul-imperiling conflict with the curse of the **Volkulak**- the beast which emerges from a man, I had been skeptical of the claims of savage peoples.

I had been skeptical as a man of science owing to the irrational and oftentimes morbid states of fascination with animals, heathen gods, and magical tales of wonder held by these children of the world. But no longer; the subject and true events of my present account passes beyond all reason. What I have seen, I cannot un-see.

In the late summer of 1893, I traveled by rail and coach to a remote eastern portion of the Bessarabia district tucked below the Ciuluc hills. While attending lectures on brain-anatomy in Prague, I was drawn by vague reports of a savage and unknown beast preying on the scattered mills and farmlands of that benighted country and upon its simple peoples. A brief study of the folklore of the region revealed the expected macabre array of vain-seeming superstitions mingled with tales of demons and the restless departed, but my experience upon arriving at my lodging, a small inn in the village of Strasenia, was out of character with the reputation of the place.

The inn was comfortable and well-arranged, and the innkeeper, one Vasily Mozgovoy, was a superlative and gracious host; he was a well-favored gentleman blessed with a faithful wife and thriving children- the oldest of which was Mariya. My inquiries into the disturbances of the mysterious creature did not meet with much conversation from my host, but the local priest of the tiny church of Saint Helen and Saint Constantin was more forthcoming for it was clear that he believed in the demonic thing called "Volkulak" by the gentry.

All of the villages in the lands of those hills had tales of it; what stood out among the tales was the grotesque nature of the beast: a twisted parody of the natural order of creatures, comprised of portions that were beast and others that were man. It went upright, but stooped when it bounded with unnatural speed; it was long of tooth and taloned, equipped with the keen senses of the predator.

The fiend slumbered by day in the form of an innocent man or woman- a hapless carrier of the curse who had no conscious awareness of their fallen state. Those whose bodies and souls housed the cursed Volkulak received it (so it was believed) from the Drazivod, an ancient god or demon of the hills and forests, whose beastly emissaries were sent upon the earth to bring God's kingdom and the world of men to ruin. I was aware before this date of legends relating to lycanthropy from haunts as far apart as Greece and Wales, but never before had I encountered legends which suggested a relationship between some ancient god or spirit, and the beastly marauder of this age. The kindly priest informed me that the Drazivod was to be equated with the devil thus hastening my understanding.

I was satisfied with the information I had acquired and happier still to travel about the nearby river-valley on horseback and speak (with the help of the before-mentioned pastor's aid) to the country-folk. I learned further that the Drazivod was a creature of eternal hunger whose attempts to devour the sun and moon thus explained, to the minds of the simple, both the occurrence of eclipses and the monthly darkening of the lunar body.

The moon, I was further told, being too stony and hard for the Drazivod's stomach, was slowly regurgitated, but it emerged from his entrails much sullied by his evil making the full moon the most wicked moon and the natural time of the Volkulak's emergence. The Volkulak-beast had the power to stalk the world for a week's time beginning with the full moon of any month.

"...What stood out among the tales was the grotesque nature of the beast: a twisted parody of the natural order of creatures, comprised of portions that were beast and others that were man..."

The moon was darkened new when I had arrived, and circumstances were such that no reports of new predation from the beast came to me while I was staying at the inn of the Vozgovoys for a long while. Nevertheless, a dense fog of fear was certainly settled across that countryside for in the month before my arrival, the Volkulak was blamed for the death of two men found gruesomely slain in lonely fields a few hours distant and south of Strasenia and for the disappearance of one small child lost near a thick stand of woods in the same locale.

It was upon the first night of the full moon that I dreamed of a terrible presence pursuing me through a dark and impenetrable forest. The terror of my dream was broken by the scream or cry of some hapless person on the streets outside of the inn. It was a woman's shriek; and though I could see nothing from my window, I pulled on my trousers and coat with desperate speed, racing for egress with nothing more than a lantern in my hands, snatched from a table in the hall outside my door. While I was in haste, I heard a sound from the dark outside that could only be described as an immense dog growling, or a pack of feral dogs arching their backs in unison, such was the strength of the din.

Downstairs, sire Mozgovoy and his wife huddled in terror along with two other travelers from parts unknown. They bade me stay, not to venture out, for certain death waited in the street, but I was compelled by the pathetic cries for help from the outside. The scientist in me also strained to know the true origin of this fantastical threat.

Outside, the moon was covered by thick clouds, and my lantern gave only a weak illumination. The piteous screams of the woman had gone silent, and I walked in the eerie stillness, straining to fathom my surroundings. As I walked nearly blind, I could describe the shape of a rugged cart in my path heavily filled with pungent hay alongside a tall building with a single light burning in its upper window. The sound of dripping water or fluid from above encouraged me to lift my lantern and strain through the night to discover the source, and as my eyes climbed higher upon the wall before me, the cloud-shrouded moon suddenly appeared bathing the world in silver light.

My earthly eyes were not prepared to receive the horror which the moonlight revealed: the torn and savaged body of a woman; her clothing shredded away exposing gore-stained legs and naked flesh. There she floated in the dark; her head and long dark hair rolling limply as something darker and more massive behind seemed to hold her aloft. The creature which was dangling her from the rooftop was impossible to make out, but undeniably covered in a layer of woolly and matted hair; its head crowned by bat-like arches of fur not unlike ragged ear-stalks.

The body of the poor woman suddenly moved through the air and collided with my person; I was cast to the ground quite stunned, and my lantern fell alongside. The beast above me sprang wide through the air and landed easily but heavily upon the stones of the road; towering as it stood and released a horrendous and harsh call into the night: a demonic roar that shook the air and made wooden shutters on windows rattle. It then lurched about with fiendish speed and locked yellow eyes upon me as I struggled in abject horror to clamber away from the bloody remains of its victim. My heart weak with panic, I dove beneath the haycart just as the creature struck out at me causing the cart to tilt and shake but sparing me for another moment.

I believed at this time that my sojourn upon this earth was finished; the fiend hurled the cart over with ease exposing me to the moon-filled sky and its towering and terrible form. A sudden commotion of cries from down the street distracted it before it could seize me and make crimson ribbons of my flesh- a large commotion, a man screaming in fear; the sound of feet pounding the stones; and a woman crying out in panic. The beast leaped away from me and towards this new commotion, and there was a loud booming crack, followed by another, followed in a few moments by the dark smell of a discharged firearm. Then only silence.

May the God of my forefathers take mercy on all those affected by the events of that terrible night! For I gathered myself, my innards weak, gasping for breath, and hurried back towards the inn only to discover a scene which inspires me to tears as I recall it again as I have recalled a hundred times since.

Vasily was on his knees, smoldering rifle cast aside, endeavoring to lift his eldest daughter Mariya from the street, and all the while his wife was shrieking, pulling at the girl's hair and arms, trying to rouse her. Mariya, knowing that her family and tenants would do nothing to aid me in my vain and fatal task, had rushed out into the perilous night to help me and had fallen victim to the Volkulak's final predatory assault of that evening. The girl lived, but had been bitten by the monster twice- once deeply on her left arm and more shallowly on the back of her youthful neck. Her dark blood pumped freely in the moonlight, rising like fountains from those fresh wounds as she gazed in shock into the darkness.

Bringing my own knowledge of medicine to bear on the injured girl for the rest of that night and into the troubled daylight of morning, I staunched the blood-flow and cleaned her injuries, aided by a local herbalist and healer hastily summoned from the corners of the village. The Mozgovoy family was inconsolable, and their dismay at me was plain for had I not hurried into the night as I had, Mariya would not have felt urged on by her conscience to follow me. But there was more in the girl's injuries which concerned them and which alarmed the folk-healer: those bitten by the Volkulak, it was believed, sometimes came to harbor their own demon within and would join in the flesh hungry moon-scourge at some point in the future.

The healer brought fresh boughs and long stems of thorned roses and made from them equal-proportioned crosses to hang over Mariya's bed and over all the windows and doors of the inn, and she boiled many strange herbs in mixture to wash the wounds and give Mariya to drink in her weakness and delirium- all attempts to keep the Volkulak-demon spirit at bay in the girl's blameless soul.

Though at the time I hoped these treatments would yield her salvation, with a heavy heart, I report now that they did not. As I stood there, a helpless witness to Mariya lying in the grip of hell and death, I was inspired to an anger and pity that I had never known before. That day, I set out single-mindedly for the destruction of this unnatural foe whose demonic reality I could not now ignore or consign to mere superstition.

I knew that my time to assay the destruction of this beast would be short; in another night's passing, the moon had already begun to diminish. In only a handful of days and nights, the fiend would fade away until another lunar cycle had replenished itself. I did not know if it would emerge again forthwith; but owing to the grimness of my surroundings and weighted down by my unbearable knowledge of the awful reality that lurked under the guise of folklore in this tormented land, I guessed that its reign of crimson mayhem would not cease unless I acted quickly. With the passing of another day, Mariya had sunk further into fever and fugue, and her constant moans of agony seared me to my core.

I spent my days with the local pastor poring over ancient maps of the province and reading all I could on the traditional weaknesses of the beast. I learned of its revulsion to the sign styled by the ancients "*Kosuny's victory emblem*", a cross of equal proportions composed of whitethorn and oak branches or twigs of equal age and thickness. The bark of a lightning-struck tree well reduced and seethed in the milk of a white cow created a brew that would torment the devil if it were cast upon him. The thorns of roses were anathema to it; but it was the force of elemental fire that could end the Volkulak with the most efficiency for its cursed frame was most vulnerable to that living, ageless substance of grace and warmth. The accounts varied with regard to its vulnerability to common steel or shot, but agreed that the demon was possessed of preternatural endurance to such things.

I spent my nights roaming about on horseback, armed with a repeating rifle and wearing about my neck the emblem of Kosuny which I speedily made from the boughs of the trees that flanked the doors of the church of Saint Helen and Saint Constantin; both planted on the same blessed feast day by the Patriarch who had consecrated the building a century ago.

A farm near Strasenia was terrorized by the Volkulak on the coming of the next evening; sheep and horses were butchered by the monster, and the son of a farmer had been laid low by the creature's talons when he boldly moved against it and attempted to dispatch it by rifle shot. A second attack on the following night was north of that ill-fated farm in a small hamlet below the mountain peak called *Kawula* by the folk there. With my time even further diminished, I strove to detect a pattern in the beast's predations. I could only divine from the church maps that the attacks occurred further and further to the north each evening. I inquired as to what was north of Kawula mountain and was told only a darkly wooded valley enclosing a small village and the ruins of an old monastery.

The monastery, now just fallen stone walls, was the very first establishment of God in these lands, the first missionary seat of an ancient bishop who carried the sign of the cross from the Christian lands south. With his brave men he faced the tide of heathen darkness in these valleys where the Volkulak and other monstrosities once walked in greater numbers.

My intuition, perhaps aided by divine providence, directed me to the conclusion that the beast was reaching out to strike at the center of God's presence in this dark realm. Its rage was reserved for all farms or hamlets that lay on the ancient road reaching north to the old church lands. I resolved to spend the coming night in the village of Kisnau beneath the hill of the ruined monastery. Taking four large, sturdy branches from the oak and whitethorns of the church, I set my horses' hooves upon the old dirt road north.

On my journey's way, I stopped by the farm of the family which had suffered the cruel loss of their son two nights before, and told them of my mission and implored their aid and blessings. The grieving mother and sisters could offer nothing to me but the sadness of their eyes; the father and remaining son showed me the devastation done by the creature and applauded my resolve.

I was heartened to realize that the cows of this farm had not been touched amid the rampage owing to the presence of a white cow in the herd, a rare blessing in these parts. I pointed this out to the farmer; and as though he was prescient of my next question, he produced two large earthenware pots of boiled milk created just as my research had told. Though this charmed milk was not able to spare his son, it had spared his family as surely as the presence of the white cow had kept the beast from his cow pasture. Taking a sheepskin full of the milk, I continued on my way.

Mariya had lost all manner of her humanity and become violent and irrational and needed to be restrained by rope in her bed and sedated by night. A formless and unbreakable darkness was settling on Strasenia and the poor hearts of Mariya's family who knew the days left on this earth with their daughter were now short.

I arrived in Kisnau as the sun began its descent to the shades below. I hurriedly endeavored to purchase a young sheep from a local farmer and rode up to the ruins of the old monastery which sat brooding over forests that had felt no woodsman's axe for many generations. Walking into the old sanctuary, now open to the dark gray sky, I took it upon myself to kneel and offer a short prayer before the ruined altar, praying for the mercies of the God of righteous men. With as much mercy and swiftness as I could, I dispatched the sheep letting its hot blood trickle from its throat all over the mossy altar and in a long trail back to my waiting horse.

Lashing the bleeding carcass behind my saddle, I rode slowly back to Kisnau leaving a crimson trail which I knew might lure the monster in only a few hours. An abandoned barn outside of the fields of Kisnau was my objective- here the contest would be decided. Dragging a few stray but massive bales of hay into the barn which maintained a solid integrity of structure despite its disuse, I cast the sheep down and rode away to fetch cans of lamp oil and a length of broad-linked chain from the sullen and suspicious folk of the village.

I soaked the bales of hay with oil then set about cutting a shaft into the stomach of the bloodless lamb before me. I filled its body with the birch-boiled milk and then made the slit good again- or as good as I could- with rough thread and a thin white bone-awl.

As the darkness fell outside, I perched on one of the beams above the wooden doors of the barn, my chain and bare knife at hand, rifle slung over my back. A small candle flickered at the end of my concealing beam; I lay as still as death glancing anxiously outside towards the old monastery towering in the distance through a well-worn hole in the timber. It seemed to me, as old night towered above, that the distant ruin began to shimmer faintly with its own luminescence.

At length, when the moon achieved mid-sky, a hideous moaning howl broke the strange stillness of the night, silencing what errant birds had dared to sing in the darkness. It began in the west, towards the poor remains of the old home of God and grew louder and more savage as the beast took up the trail of blood left by me. My heart pounded as the moonlight revealed a great dark shape racing towards the barn in which I sat, my whole body twitching with a nerve-ruining mixture of dread and excitement.

As surely as hell's vengeance, the stride of the beast carried him into the barn and directly beneath my perch where it sniffed loudly at the sheep's carcass and seized it. Though I could not see what transpired then, I know that the Volkulak must have taken a greedy tear from the sheep's corpse, and been rewarded with a geyser of the holy milk which seared its mouth and eyes with a terrible vengeance.

I didn't spare a moment to revel in the symphony of horrible sounds that spewed forth from the dripping maw of the creature; I seized the candle and cast it below upon the bales of hay, and just as the flames burst good into blaze, I dropped to the earth with my knife and chain, landing poorly.

The pains that lanced through the sinews of my leg were not enough to overcome my zeal, nor my fear-laced certainty that the lumbering, shrieking monstrosity who writhed in misery but ten feet from my back would recover to seek vengeance. I dashed to the doors of the barn and dragged them closed. I pulled the chain through the thick metal rings on either door and thrust my knife through the links, as tight as I could manage, just as a great force from within made the doors buckle heavily. The monster shrieked and roared like the entire choir of the abyss- I fought the strong urge to press my hands over my ears to block out even a little of the damnable noise.

The fire inside the barn had now spread to the other haybales; the golden light pouring from within, and the thick plumes of smoke forcing their way from the cracks told the story well. I stumbled backwards, unslung my rifle, and began to retreat from the barn. I began desperately praying to the good Christ that the beast would be cowed by the flames and not able to force his way through the wooden walls.

But God in his unknowable wisdom had other plans for this terrible evening; though my heart fluttered with hope as the devilish howls of the beast within became shrieks of pain, the northern wall of the barn exploded and the monster emerged, its eyes full of murder and its stinking hide draped in flames. Swift as a devil, it began to run erratically through the fallow fields for the nearby forest-wall. I got off a wild and panicked shot at it, re-chambered and began running as fast as I could after the beast. The nauseating smell of its burned hair and flesh was everywhere; and though injured, it made a diabolical pace towards the sanctuary of the forest.

I knew I wouldn't match it before it made the shelter of the grim trees so I stopped, drew my ragged breath inside me and aimed as carefully as I could; my arm trembling and heart pounding. It was then that I knew God's grace had finally arrived, for in one strange and peaceful moment, with Mariya's face in my mind, I knew a calmness which steadied my aim and my shot was true. The beast rolled forward from the impact and struggled to stand.

I ran forward another fourteen paces and lined up a second shot. The beast had stood, but my next bullet shattered the thing's spine. It fell forward and appeared to try to crawl, making a guttural groan. The fury of the fire in the barn had truly weakened the devil; but still I knew that these bullets of heavy lead would not prevail to end the creature. As it began to rise again, I arrived alongside it and began to smash its skull again and again with my rifle, wielding it as a club.

This was not the end of my struggle; after taking three crushing blows, the beast burst forward with an unexpected surge of strength, barreling into me and throwing me at least ten feet backwards into a thick trough of mud. My bloodstained rifle sailed off into darkness, and the beast lumbered about, confused, looking for my flesh. Its hateful eyes raked over me, lying in the dark, tense but still- and when my moment was good, I let out a cry to regain my courage and dashed to where I hoped my rifle would be. It was as I hoped, and I grasped it sturdily just as the monster reached me. My wild swing was blessed; the creature buckled as its face shattered, and it fell to the ground before me.

I think the toll of the creature's gruesome burns are what finally brought it to ground; taking the time to fire from instinct range, I discharged all the bullets I had left into the creature's head and neck, as well as I could see them, till only a tattered ruin remained there. Under the now strong moonlight, I could see that the burned and savaged body of the Volkulak became that of a man- though what face God gave him at birth was long burned and shot away. Neither myself nor the people of this lonely country would ever know who carried the curse that cost them so dearly.

"...The northern wall of the barn exploded and the monster emerged, its eyes full of murder and its stinking hide draped in flames."

With the passing of the Volkulak from this world, Mariya's fits and struggles ceased, but she never regained consciousness enough to speak thereafter- she lay still, her breathing shallow for the three days and nights it took her to finally respire her last. I was there at her bedside when her soul fled to God; I slumped back in the chair near her bed and prayed as earnestly as I could that her innocent soul would be in the safekeeping of Heaven, safe from any detestable power that could pursue it to its hurt ever again.

Her final serenity was evident on her face; my own serenity, like that of her parents, would not find us; we feared for many years to come, if it found us at all.

***

THE BELIEVERS

***

In no manner do I consider myself prone to entertaining fantastical ideas especially those straying in the direction of supernaturalism or superstition. I am a psychiatrist; the realm of mental illness is both my deepest interest as well as a thing I have a mandate to study and understand. I seek this understanding so that I can help to alleviate the immeasurable pain that mental illness causes in as many people as I may.

Disturbances of the mind take many forms. When those disturbances reach an intensity sufficient to imprison people in the depths of true delusion, it is fair to say that they are trapped by two cognitive prisons not one. The first prison is whatever terrible maladaptation of biology and perception actually delivers them to their inability to grasp reality. The second prison is found in the way their own delusions seem (to them) so lucidly normal and unquestionable. No man or woman can free themselves from a prison they do not believe they are in.

Having been clinician to many, I know how important it is to maintain absolute objectivity in the face of vibrant delusions and to rely upon the literature of my field. An untrained mind exposed to the relentless energy and sincerity with which the mentally ill are devoted to their delusions might easily wonder if there was something to the incredible things these people say.

One day, and rather unexpectedly, this lesson became clear to me: a patient and I were enjoying a simple conversation by the window on the fourth floor of Millbrook when she gestured out to the thick flock of grackles that was perched on the upper branches of a crooked hawthorn. "There they are," she said, "though they look so different now."

I pressed her further on what she meant, and she told me about the "circle of angels" that had visited her and told her about the secret purpose of her life. They waited for her now to join them, sometimes appearing as faces gazing through the window of her room when she lay in bed at night, or sometimes in the bathroom mirror; and at times, as ordinary-seeming birds, like these grackles, gently singing to her in tones only she could hear.

It was the look of serene conviction in her eyes, such utter peace; she wasn't displaying a faith to me but a deep certainty. She was not harmed by this certainty; she was greatly uplifted by it, transformed into a stronger person. At that moment, some part of me wanted to join her in this vision of otherworldly entities and mystical birds; I wanted to be lifted up like her. For the briefest of seconds, I imagined what it would be like to believe her. I could imagine, in some fleeting way, that a better world was possible or closer somehow- a world full of real meaning.

I didn't join her in her delusion, obviously, nor did I offer any reinforcement to it, but I felt ashamed in some way. It seemed shameful, at least on the surface, that I would secretly work to remove this source of peace from her. But these angels of hers were not mere messengers of peace; her schizoaffectivity caused many issues in her family and social life beyond and had rendered her incapable of living on her own. The strength of her convictions- whatever their source- didn't translate into the minimum strength required to maintain life in our social world; this patient had nearly starved herself to death before she was committed to Millbrook.

Upon reflection, I came to a better appreciation of the elusive psychological mechanisms at work behind the growth and maintenance of religious cults and sects. To experience another person manifesting such perfect sincerity and peace lures the deeper and less-than-rational parts of us towards the display in a very subtle (and I would say insidious) manner. I am as inured to this danger now as I have always been. I have always taken note of my personal feelings, examined them, remained objective, and held to proper treatment courses for all my patients.

But the strange workings of the mind, from their most deceptive to their most perverse, never cease to amaze me. One can never become too comfortable, and there's always room to be surprised.

* * *

When Melissa H. became one of my patients, it was not the first time I had worked in conjunction with the court system. But it was the first time a patient of mine had such notoriety; she was the defendant in a murder case that had attracted great media attention. Found guilty but not culpable for her actions on the grounds of an acute episode of mental illness, she was committed indefinitely to Millbrook and passed into my care. It was immediately obvious that whatever delusions Melissa H. maintained, they were not of the sort that lent themselves to serenity. For nine months, she never spoke a word to myself nor any of the staff at Millbrook. Her affect was low; she was largely catatonic, but the torment in her eyes was plainly visible and it never subsided. It was a very frustrating period for me personally.

Melissa H., age 44, (aged 41 at the time of the commission of her crimes) was a tenured professor of Anthropology, Archaeology and Early New England Studies at Cranwick University in Haverhill. Nothing in her long and prestigious academic background could ever have suggested such a dark outcome for her life, and neither she nor anyone else in her family has a known history of mental illness.

In response to the need to utilize the funds of an extremely generous temporary grant, the university gained permission to excavate and study the remains of a colonial settlement in northern New Hampshire which was discovered on a large and remote estate in 2006. The Yeaver family, who owned the estate, also paid generously for the effort.

"For nine months, she never spoke a word to myself nor any of the staff at Millbrook. Her affect was low, she was largely catatonic, but the torment in her eyes was plainly visible and it never subsided."

The settlement, as it turned out, was the remain of a commune occupied by the reclusive Harsonite sect, an early American religious group led by Harson Hale who had established a community there in 1777. This period of history and particularly the fringe religious and social movements of the time was the focus of Melissa H's graduate and doctoral work. She was chosen to head up this excavation and study on those grounds as her previous excavation work in other parts of New England, Quebec, and Florida had won her an enormous amount of respect in her field.

In 2008, the excavation and study of the site was well underway. In the summer of 2011, Melissa H. vanished from her own life, from her university and any contact with her family, and dropped off the map entirely. A fellow academic and co-leader of the excavation and study named Henry McAllister had likewise vanished some months before. He was discovered brutally murdered along with two other persons (Margaret Cabot and Scott Hill) who had worked on the excavation at a cabin not far from the excavation site. Melissa H. had apparently bludgeoned McAllister to death with a log and battered his remains until his entire head was disarticulated and destroyed. She had shot Cabot and Hill before that point and returned to batter their corpses until they too were effectively headless at some point later.

She attempted to burn the cabin down with their remains still inside but only managed to damage it before local responders brought the blaze under control. Melissa H. was found 12 hours later in the forest three miles from the cabin, in a highly agitated state, attempting to flee.

Throughout her incarceration, her meetings with doctors and clinicians, her trial, and for nine months after she came through the door of Millbrook, Melissa H. never said a word. The only explanation for her actions were documents saved on her laptop which detailed- in an intricate, nearly incomprehensible manner- how she believed McAllister was no longer a human being, and further, that he had enticed

Cabot and Hill into some kind of procedure that would remove their humanity as well, transforming them into dangerous creatures (albeit very human-looking ones.)

Special permission to see the actual documents from the laptop wasn't easy to come by; but highlights had been typed up for an evidentiary presentation, and I looked over those. I had obtained them within a month of Melissa H's committal. I wanted very much to understand how this fantastical, and ultimately deadly narrative, had arisen in the first place. I wished to fathom what strange fields of cause and effect had come together to precipitate its initial formation and then upheld its growth and elaboration. I needed to hear Melissa H. talk about it, to hear how she rationalized it and defended it. But her lips were closed.

* * *

The only way I could think to bring my patient out of her shell was to find common ground and appeal to the dominant features of her person- her intellect, and her lifetime of fruitful engagement in the world of academia and science. The acute disassociation from reality that had destroyed her life began around the time of her excavation of the Harsonite commune and her specialty area of knowledge dealt with early American religious movements. So I began to research the Harsonites, and largely with Melissa H's unknowing help. My main source of information was written by her very hands; a scholarly study of the Harsonite sect published in an academic journal online entitled "The Believers: The Harsonite Sect and Helio-Arkite Worship in Colonial America."

Both the region of New England and New York state in the 18th and 19th centuries were fertile ground for alternative religious movements and the formation of strange cults and sects. The most famous of these new religious movements is still with us and thriving: The Mormon church. The "Latter Day Saints" (as they call themselves) were sprung from the purported visions of a man claiming to have been visited by an angel who gave him miraculous gems or spectacles that allowed him to translate the writing on golden plates from an unknown "reformed Egyptian" language into the language of the popular King James Bible- plates which the same angel guided him to uncover from the ground near his home in New York state.

The plates contained (so the story goes) a lost history of ancient Semitic tribes- lost tribes of Israel- who had crossed the Atlantic Ocean and settled in North America. Melissa H's study mentioned the Mormons at some length as an example of a cult based on a certain motif that has a deep home in English and American folklore: the idea of ancient peoples from the Near East or Europe crossing the Atlantic Ocean and establishing civilizations or settlements in North America. The legendary voyage of St. Brendan was also mentioned as a lesser reflex of the same myth.

Several heretical groups in England, from at least the 18th century onward, have believed in a pseudo-historical body of myths called by scholars the "Helio-Arkite" belief system. It posits that Noah's ark was not really an actual boat; it was a boat-shaped temple to the sun god or to a mysterious divinity symbolized by the sun and called the "True Jehovah." Noah himself was seen by the proponents of the Helio-Arkite religion as a primordial priest or mystic who knew the secrets of the true God by which righteousness could be established on earth and within human societies. Noah's "sons" were those men initiated by him into the true religion, who then endeavored to sail around Europe and Africa in their "Sun Arks" while others journeyed overland into Asia, to spread their creed to early humanity.

In England, the before-mentioned heretical groups often believed that the ancient Druid priests of the British Isles were initiatory descendants of the Noahite priesthood, that had come to the isles in prehistory, in sacred ships with the sign of the sun emblazoned on their sails. Throughout history, until the coming of Christianity, the true "Druidic Religion" (they believed) was a solar-oriented monotheism.

Further, this was their explanation for why the druids supposedly converted to the new faith with such readiness and alacrity: they saw in the new religion the culmination of the Helio-Arkite solar monotheism which taught immortality for the soul in exchange for righteous behavior. The British Helio-Arkites of the 18th and 19th centuries also believed that "lost tribes of Israel" had come to Britain to settle there and became ancestors of the British people.

This historical background was fascinating enough all on its own, but when the details came on the Harsonite movement in colonial Massachusetts and New Hampshire, it became much more intriguing.

* * *

Harson Edward Hale was born in 1744 in western Massachusetts; the son of a farmer who was also a country preacher and minister named Obadiah Hale and his wife, Aphra. Conflicts with the Abenaki Natives in the region had been fierce just twenty years before Harson's birth, but only small holdout groups of Natives still conducted raids on English farms and settlements by 1740. Obadiah chose to live in a dangerous and secluded place partly because he was intent on ministering to the "diminished heathen people" and not simply shooting at them.

One night (or so the legend cited by Melissa H. recounted) a war party overran Obadiah's farm, and the only thing that spared him, his wife, and his infant son from certain and painful doom was Obadiah's total lack of fear in the face of the bloody brave who led the attack. The brave took Obadiah to a holy man of the Abenaki believing that Obadiah had some strange form of magic that rendered him invulnerable to the brave's own war magic.

This holy man was feared far and wide and had become known as "The Red Woodman" by the English on account of his power to inspire other Natives into bloody assaults on the English colonists, but also for the fact that he was believed to live a solitary life away from the other natives deep in the forests. When Obadiah re-emerged safe and sound from his captivity among the Natives, it was declared a miracle. Obadiah claimed that he had "by the grace of God befriended the holy man of the heathens"- and indeed, as the years passed, he spent a lot of time away from his farm and among the people of the Red Woodman.

By the time Harson Hale was eleven years old, his father had been greatly transformed by his association with the Natives. Not only Obadiah's person and character, but the nature of his beliefs had changed radically. He had begun to preach strange things to the small congregation that came to him- stories of what he called the "true religion of Noah" and how it had been carried just a few years after the crucifixion of Jesus to the coast of Massachusetts by ancient Britons who were fleeing the scourge of Rome.

Obadiah said that the Britons, led by a "righteous druid" named Cadoc, had crossed the ocean and come among the natives 2000 years ago, bringing to them "the religion of that won for men immortality"- a pure version of the true religion that certain groups among the Natives had been practicing ever since. Obadiah believed that this transmission of Noahite religion, which had been in the keeping of the Natives for so many centuries, was unstained and unsullied by the "corruptions of cleric and monarch" that had diminished the ordinary Christianity of his time.

The things he began to teach people were so strange that most abandoned him. Some called him a witch, or claimed that his time among the heathens had cost him his soul. The few believers who rallied around him were devoted to his vision of a true and lost religion that could alone "summon the soul from the body and endow it with immortality." The original "Believers", as they called themselves, lived on Obadiah's land with his family and don't appear to have numbered more than thirty men, women, and children.

By the time of the beginning of the Revolutionary War, Obadiah disappears from all records, and a thirty-year-old Harson Hale is the clear leader of the sect that history remembers as the "Harsonites." Harson led his congregation, which by then numbered some 300 souls, into the mountains of northern New Hampshire. This exodus was undertaken perhaps to evade the troubles of the war, but certainly to carry on their practice of the "ancient and true religion" in secrecy and seclusion.

"Secretive and secluded" described the Harsonites well; only a handful of them ever left their commune, and then only twice a year, at which time they traded large quantities of honey and beeswax along with hides and other goods and returned to their settlement. No outsiders were ever allowed in, and only second-hand reports of the layout or appearance of their community exist in records.

The expected dark rumors began, of course, with Harson Hale being accused (among other things) of dissolving all marriages and sexually dominating his congregation, siring endless bastard children on the hapless women and so forth. Rumors of heathen worship, animal sacrifice, and even human sacrifice circulated about, too. The fact that the Harsonite community was never attacked or bothered by Natives seemed to justify the dangerous heathen associations. The Harsonites refused to recognize or accept the authority of any state, declaring themselves "free and unsullied."

And that's apparently how it went until 1815, when the traders from Harson's village didn't appear. They didn't come the next year either; and when a party from Concord went north into the mountains, they found the settlement overgrown, and all its buildings burned to the ground. There was no trace of anyone who used to live there, alive or dead. No explanation for this was ever discovered or even suggested. The location of the Harsonite commune was forgotten, and American history gained another unsolved mystery for future generations to ponder.

* * *

It was a bright Monday morning, and I was sitting across from Melissa H. in the west wing therapy room preparing to play my hand. I told her how impressed I was that she spent two long years digging in the ground at the Harsonite archaeological site, and how interested I was in knowing if anything she had unearthed had given her some idea of the cause of the community's disappearance. I styled myself an avid student of the unsolved mysteries of American history and had just begun to regale her with my own theories about what became of the missing colonists at Roanoke when she interrupted me.

In my stunned and sudden silence, she apologized to me, quietly, with a half-choked, halting voice. She apologized for ignoring me and refusing to speak for all these months. "I just had to be sure", she kept saying.

She wouldn't tell me what she was trying to be so certain of. I didn't press the issue; I was too happy that she had broken her wall of silence and didn't want to put pressure on her in any way.

Trying to keep the friendly tone of the initial conversation going; and laboring to make myself seem as little like a psychiatrist as I could, I questioned her again about the subject of the vanished Harsonites and the results of her various excavations.

She asked me then to write something down. I eagerly wrote down a name she gave me- Alice Hopkins- and a phone number. She said that Alice was her closest colleague and friend at Cranwick, though she had no idea what Alice must be thinking of her now, in light of all that had happened. She told me to call Alice; she said that I had her permission to reveal that I was a psychiatrist attending to her in Millbrook. She said that Alice would have access to all of her dig and excavation notes and documents of findings from the Harsonite commune project. She wanted me to obtain them.

I wondered aloud why she should want me to have them, or if she intended for me to obtain them for her. She told me that she was prepared to reveal everything to me- everything that had happened, and everything I could wish to know, but she said that she could never simply reveal what she had to say from across a table. She said that her story and her explanation for her actions would only convince me further that she was hopelessly insane. "But if you see what

I saw" she continued, "If you understand it the way I came to understand it, you will be able to truly grasp the reality of the situation. Then it won't matter what you think about me."

Giving her whatever she needed to feel capable of making this detailed explanation of her actions was, I believed, the key to bringing Melissa H. closer to personal therapeutic insight. Getting archaeological field notes from her expedition was a small matter; an easy price I was willing to pay happily. I told her I would do my best to obtain what she wanted before the end of the week. She seemed to make a short, tiny hint of a smile, but it was gone before I could be sure. I smiled back myself, and there was no need to act pleased; I was genuinely overjoyed. "So, will your notes help me to understand what happened to the Harsonites?" I asked, eager to continue the alliance-making small talk.

Her haunted eyes suddenly moved and fixed on me from within the boundaries of her solemn face, and she uttered a single word at a little more than a whisper:

"Yes."

* * *

Alice Hopkins, whose trinket-and-display-case crammed office I found myself sitting in two mornings later, was very friendly. Alice was of indeterminate age, perhaps fifty, perhaps older. Her glasses had strange but stylish teardrop-shaped lenses. She was deeply concerned about Melissa, and couldn't restrain herself from asking me many questions that I couldn't answer for reasons of confidentiality. I assured her that my patient's treatment was proceeding well and explained that Melissa wanted to share her excavation notes and discoveries with me. I explained that such acts of sharing and bonding were a means to create the alliance needed for more therapeutic activities and conversations in the future.

Alice was very accommodating. I drove away from Cranwick with all my seats covered in stacks of folders and boxes. Ordinarily such documentation wouldn't be allowed out with a stranger so easily; but Melissa H. had never gotten the chance to officially study and re-examine all of her findings. She had never written an analysis on the various lab results nor created the narrative needed to bring it all together. She had vanished before that point. Without expert analysis and presentation, her notebooks and all these gathered records were destined to sit idle in the basement of Ephraim Parsons Hall.

A day later, Melissa H. was opening the boxes and thumbing through them, pulling out file folders and putting them aside. She unfolded a large grid-marked poster that was a map of the entire excavation site and laid it out on the table before me. She wasn't talking much, and I didn't want to talk too much so I just sat by smiling good naturedly and preparing to take notes.

She told me about the discovery of the site- how the hikers who had found it only came across the exposed, moss-covered foundation stones of seven central buildings. They were built on the north-south axis of the site, side by side.

Each of them was rectangular, measuring 80 feet on their long sides and 25 feet on their short sides. Of the seven, the fourth (the center building with three buildings on either side of it) was 120 feet long by 35 feet. All of these structures were 30 feet apart. They all faced east.

About 15 feet behind the central house, a large, narrow boulder- which Melissa H. said was a standing stone intentionally lifted into place there- was positioned and still standing upright though silt and dirt had piled up maybe two feet around its base where the open ground was centuries ago. She was able to indicate on the map where all these features were.

She said these houses- with the central house likely being the home of Harson Hale- were communal living buildings, done in a strange "longhouse" style and likely having multiple floors. There were cellars dug into the earth as well, though all of the cellars were filled when they found the site. These seven houses were not the only residential buildings, but they were certainly the first built at the site. Six more "longhouses" were found though they were considerably smaller: three of them were found about 400 feet south of the central area, and the other three were 400 feet north of the central area.

On the map, Melissa showed me a long oval-shaped boundary of big black dots surrounding the main house at the very center of the site. These were filled-in pits, she explained, that she and her colleagues had once thought held large wooden posts, but later they discovered that they held more upright stones like the one still standing behind the house. When the site was occupied, the house was surrounded by an oval of very heavy standing stones, each of the stones being about 15 feet apart.

From the pressure of the vanished stones on the impacted soil below, it was determined that the two tallest and heaviest stones were the ones directly in front of the house, and the one still standing behind it. The others were shorter, but each one weighed nearly 1500 pounds. The two tallest stones (based on the one still standing) weighed roughly 2000 pounds. When I asked where they got their big stones, she said that they were glacial erratics; many of which are scattered in the forests of that region and around settlements.

Thinking of the Helio-Arkite obsession with the druids and Britain, I joked about Harson having a "Stonehenge" around his house. Melissa looked at me blankly and said that it was no henge. She said the stones were arranged in their oval shape, with a tall front stone and a tall back one, to represent a boat. I was intrigued.

"Their boat-temple also contained the living space of their leader and high priest, Harson Hale" she said. "But we didn't realize the extent of the site for at least two months until we found their symbolic sun. It was mapped onto the ground, onto the entire site of their community."

She showed me on the excavation map. "We knew that everything we had excavated so far was on a north-south axis. But there was an east-west axis, as well. And it contained sites and artifacts, too." She pointed to a symbol on the map again. "This tree was there at the time of the original settlement- and it is directly east of the main house, about 100 feet out. It's the oldest tree on the site."

"When the Harsonites came to the site of the commune, they cut down the original forest. They cut into the woodland, making an enormous circular clearing, and used the wood for their first buildings at the very center of the site. For whatever reason, they left this one tree standing. They only built structures on the north-south axis of the site, or on the east-west axis. The large open spaces between were clearly used for communal gardens or keeping animals pinned. It was hard to understand this at first because the entire site has become reclaimed by the forest."

I moved my eyes up and down the map, scanning to see if the east-west axis, which was marked in light blue on the map, contained other markers for sites. It did. Directly behind the tree to the east of the main house were found two graves but both empty, and their stones intentionally damaged by someone to make them unreadable. Beyond them, another small hut had stood. Where the eastern edge of the commune clearing was, another glacial erratic was moved and erected, but it was found fallen on its side. The other terminal of this axis had no great stone nor did the other axis-terminals. The entire site was laid out like an enormous equal-armed cross, a solar cross, as Melissa described it- with their "boat" at the center; its bow pointing towards the eastern sunrise and the big stone that probably marked it.

I told Melissa that I had read her paper regarding the Harsonites. I mentioned the honey and beeswax that they traded. She told me that some of the open spaces of the massive clearing might have contained beehives, but no evidence for that had been uncovered. Bees, however, had shown up at the site.

Their first safety incident had occurred when one of the student workers sustained multiple bee stings at one of the houses on the southern axis. Unlike all the other buildings, its floorboards were not made from wood but stone slabs. This meant that the cellar space was still hollow and preserved, and due to a small collapse of the earth, the space below ground had been open to the surface for some years. Bees had turned the entire cellar into a hive of immense proportions. This had caused work to cease at the site for two weeks until exterminators painstakingly cleared the hive.

* * *

This talk about the excavation and its discoveries went on for two weeks. I was always interested in what my patient had to say; and despite my real focus being elsewhere, my knowledge of the excavation and its many intricacies grew exponentially. Finally, late one Friday afternoon, Melissa pointed to a spot on the map that was in the forest beyond the limits of the old settlement and another 100 feet or so east of the large eastern stone.

"We thought it was a Native burial mound" she said. "But I had a hunch that it was positioned on the eastern axis, but outside of the settled boundaries for a reason. I excavated it. It wasn't Native; it was something the Harsonites built. What looked like a very large mound of earth, dark green and grown-over, had begun as a small, square structure of logs, maybe four feet high and six feet square, which had then been covered completely with a cairn of hundreds of stones, and then earth had been piled over the cairn."

I didn't have a chance to ask if someone had been buried in the mound, though that was my first thought.

"I opened the central chamber myself, and what we found was beyond any possible expectation. There were two blocks of what looked like yellow stone, but they turned out to be large blocks of beeswax. We dated the construction of the mound to the late 1700's based on debris in the ground of the chamber and in the lower levels of fill. Harsonites were the creators. Even though the oxygen level in the central chamber was low, beeswax shouldn't have lasted that long without decaying more. But these yellow blocks were so strong that it took us time to realize they were actually wax. Lab analysis turned up traces of something mixed into the wax that couldn't be identified but must have been added in as a preservative of some kind."

Melissa H's mood had changed. She was no longer matter-of-fact; she seemed withdrawn. I took notice of this shift- not that it could be missed- and guessed that the details of this mysterious mound were not mere archaeological details, but factors that led to the terrible events to come.

"Inside the first block of beeswax we found a container of birch-bark that held a strange silver cup made from what I thought was a mixture of tin and some other kind of metals, but we could never be sure. Tests there were inconclusive, as well. The cup was strange, maybe six inches high, 8 inches wide at its lip, marked around its rim with patterns and lozenges and spirals, not unlike the "grooved ware" patterns they find on pottery in British Neolithic finds. It was clearly very old, but we were unable to date it. The other block of beeswax had another container of birch wood, but it held nine hard, round balls of some kind of organic material. They were dark brown in color, maybe an inch and a half in diameter. We had mistook them for small stones initially before a test showed that they were something else."

I had expected more from this revelation. Melissa H. had gone quiet. Eager to keep her talking, I questioned her as to what she thought they were used for. She didn't respond; then I noticed that she was shaking a bit, and tears had begun to run down her cheeks. I did not react with shock; I quietly offered her a tissue, and told her in my most gentle voice that we could take a break if she wanted.

But she did not want a break. She took a deep breath and said "Maggie and Scott were innocent, they weren't corrupted. I didn't know that, and I couldn't risk it. They died human deaths. I might have... saved them from something worse. But Henry was no longer Henry. I shot him. I shot him at least four times, including once in his head, but he didn't die. I had to destroy his head completely, just... completely. It was horrible. But I was so scared."

My throat had gone dry and my heart was pounding so hard I thought sure Melissa would hear it. "What was wrong with Henry?" I asked. "What had happened to him?"

"We called the stone-floored house "the beehive" after the discovery of the immense hive under it. Greg Dalley, the student worker who was stung, nearly died. Henry was assigned the excavation of the beehive after it was safe. The cellar of that house was the only sub-surface structure that had survived intact. He dug some pits in the floor, and found another one of the yellow blocks of beeswax. Inside of this one was a birch-bark box that contained a book- a book written by Harson Hale, in a perfect state of preservation. Only... the writer of the book didn't call himself Harson Hale. He said that he had begun his life as Harson Hale, but now he had achieved immortality and become an entity named Shul-Ezkor."

I was starting to feel very strange. My mind was racing in fifteen different directions at once. I didn't know what to say and Melissa seemed to be drifting away. "That's very strange, indeed!" I suddenly said. "Do you think that Hale had taken a new name, a religious name, after some kind of religious ritual that he believed made him immortal?"

Melissa H. fixed me again with her gaze; but this time, it was dangerous looking. "He didn't believe he was immortal.

He was immortal. He may still be. The book detailed everything about how he became what he became. It detailed what the Red Woodman had taught his father, Obadiah. It talked about the wise man who came from over the ocean- Cadoc and all his people- and how he taught the Natives about the Goddess Shul-Nagorath, She who brought all life into being as mortal, corruptible forms, and the spirit Ceidiaw or Ceadio who made life immortal and put it beyond corruption."

Her eyes were burning into me now. "I saw the drawings in the book, I know what they were doing in their fields- I saw the pole crowned with the black goat's head, and the hide banner hanging from it, stitched with the heads of countless other creatures. They worshiped it, worshiped her, their Goddess. They did terrible things to secure her blessings. I found the remains of their celebrations. People must celebrate and accept the corrupt and mortal things of life before they can journey to the immortal, the book said. Cadoc knew how to pull the soul from the body and make it immortal. It was the druid-eggs that made it possible. The book gave instructions for the whole ritual. The things we thought were stones were eggs. They were to be dissolved in water, in the special cup, and the initiate drank it all down."

I realized that I was losing control of the conversation, and that Melissa H's emotional state was spiraling rapidly into a dangerous place. I tried to get her mind off of the contents of this book, and back to some more mundane detail. "And you authenticated this book? I mean, did you turn it in? Is it at Cranwick? It wasn't among the things Mrs. Hopkins gave to me."

It was like she hadn't heard a word I said. "They who drink, die. It's poison; it's a neurotoxin; it paralyzes... and kills. But there is some kind of... DNA or something in it; a parasite, it takes maybe a week, sometimes up to three weeks, but it grows inside their bodies, it steals their genetic material, bodily fluids... it grows and finally emerges. Shul-Ezkor sketched it, the very image of the soul when it is summoned from the body. But... I saw it, I saw them, with my own eyes. It is... they are... just over a foot long but dark brown, leathery, they have six long legs, spider-like legs... flesh-shaped protrusions on the back, like wings, but they do not fly. They run; they dart with great rapidity; and they have mandibles, or teeth, it's impossible to explain. I saw no eyes, but they can sense everything around them..."

She did stare at me and hung on my words like she was devouring them. She had a wild and fearful gaze that filled me with dread, despite all my attempts to maintain my own calm. Slowly, she sat down.

I started to talk again, but she cut me off. "You need to know; you need to know; you need to know" is all she said, over and over again. I put my hand on hers and it seemed to shock her a bit. "You need to know that these things are real" she said.

"I saw the pole crowned with the black goat's head, and the hide banner hanging from it, stitched with the heads of countless other creatures."

"They run away; they burrow into the ground or maybe into trees; but after a while, they send out big black growths that look like tree stumps or dark, leafless trees. Then they open, and what comes out looks exactly like the person who drank the solvent and died. But it isn't them anymore. It's a thing, a monster, but it can pass for human; it has at least some or maybe most of the memories of the person it hosted from. They are very strong, beyond strong, and intelligent. They cough up... or produce these druid eggs from inside their throats and hide them.

Cadoc... the Red Woodman... Obadiah... Hale... all his people- those who took the drink from the cup, they are still out there. The book- the book says that one day, Shul-Ezkor, like all the other immortals, will "go among them below"- he meant a cave. There are caves; one series of caves is actually close to the commune site- and as the Believers were transformed one by one, they went to live down in the caverns. After a while, I mean. Some of the reborn stayed, and they were... like gods. Mortal humans are Shul-Nagorath's beings. The Believers became Ceidiaw 's beings. It's all there; all in the book."

She was seeming quite disturbed; I finally had to push back. "It's just a book. Religious people can be very crazy, say and do crazy things. But they believe things, and they can be very convincing in that belief."

"Henry read the book too. He found it; he helped decipher it. He drank one of the dissolved eggs" she said. I stopped. "He died. That thing, it came out of him, and later... Henry, the thing that re-appeared claiming to be Henry, it wasn't him. I hid, but he found me. I saw. I saw the thing. I saw a monster that bullets couldn't kill that looked like Henry. He was going to make me drink. He was going to make Scott and Maggie drink- Scott and he were best friends, and Scott even helped him... early on. But Scott and Maggie didn't. They didn't know what was really going on."

I had the sinking realization then that there was going to be no easy solution to the delusional world of Melissa H. She had confessed to a triple murder in front of me in the space of a few hours. She had never talked about this, nor confessed, to anyone before. Some would have considered this a therapeutic breakthrough of the highest order, but I felt nothing but confusion and a deep hint of fear.

"Where is the book now?" I asked her.

"The monster that masqueraded as Henry took it away somewhere; I have no idea where, but I can guess into one of the caves" she replied without looking at me. "And the other things... the strange cup? The druid eggs?" She looked up at me then.

"I carried the cup and the remaining eggs away from the cabin after I killed the thing. I headed south, and about a hundred paces straight down the slope from the cabin, there was a strong tree jutting out with a deep hollow. I put them all in there. They might still be there. If you could get them... but no, you can't because no one should be in that forest. The... Believers might still come up from the caves at night, or during the day. They can pass as human; they seem as human as you or I. They could be living anywhere, acting normal, seeming normal."

"But if I did get this cup and these eggs- what do you think it could prove?"

"I don't know- someone could really analyze one of the eggs, DNA sequence it, something. It is a life-form that is unknown, unprecedented, and dangerous. It would show you that I'm not crazy."

"Why were the cup and eggs not turned in with the rest of your findings?" I asked. "Henry took them, took it all, and ran with it. He believed what he saw in the book. He wanted me to help him to see if there was anything to it, but I wouldn't. Not after a point."

* * *

I had vacation time saved up. I had a good deal of it, in fact, living life perpetually single, as I do, means that you don't have many people to take on nice vacations, and I hate doing fun things alone. I took off the time, and I went to the forest, went to the still-vacant cabin which was the crime scene, and tried to find Melissa H's tree; the place she claimed she stashed the special cup and the demonic eggs. I know what you're thinking already: this is over-involvement; this is very silly, rash, or stupid; this is giving way to the delusions of patients; I know. I've heard it all. I've even said it all to certain among my colleagues when I saw them doing similar things over the years.

And yet, there I was. I admit I was creeped out a bit by Melissa's story. I didn't believe it, but she was so sincere... so very sincere. Some part of me, against my own conscious will, was trying to believe her. And right in the middle of this struggle between the rational and irrational parts of my being; on a wooded road early in the day, my car made a loud sound, died, and rolled to a stop. I looked under the hood- not that I know anything about what's under the hoods of cars- but saw nothing and could make nothing work.

"...They are... just over a foot long, but dark brown, leathery, they have six long legs, spider-like legs... flesh-shaped protrusions on the back, like wings, but they do not fly."

I must have sat in my car for at least two hours, occasionally frantically trying the key over and over again, until I finally abandoned that idea. I walked after that. It was later afternoon by the time I made it to the crime scene. The other two cabins in the area were also unoccupied. I stood on the boundary of the property, looking down the steep incline that led away into the dark woods. I looked back at the cabin and tried to visualize where Melissa H. would have walked out that night and started her descent south. I looked at my compass, lined myself up on a likely trajectory, and started heading down.

I found the tree. It wasn't hard to find- it was slightly darker than the other trees not that Melissa would have been able to tell that at night. And it had a perfectly round hole in its trunk; a hole that led into inky blackness. I shined my flashlight in, but I still couldn't make out anything. The very last thing I wanted to do was stick my hand and arm into the hole, but I finally got the courage and did it. And my hand felt something smooth, hard, and cold.

It was a cup, a strange silvery cup, almost pewter looking, but very heavy in the hand and carved with odd symbols.

A snapping sound in the forest sent me into a startled head-circling, but I saw nothing. I looked back at the hole in the tree, and right then, the most unsettling sensation of someone or something watching me began to assault my entire being. I calmed myself- I remembered the words of my rational self- this was New Hampshire, not the Haunted Forest of some fairy tale- and I looked around.

There was a man standing up the slope of the forested ridge from me. He couldn't have been more than fifteen or twenty paces from me. He was so still, I might have walked right by him before, or passed my eyes right over him in my glancing around. He was as still as a tree or a stone. He seemed to my sight to be Native American- his skin tone was dark, and I remember it as reddish or dark brown. The look in his face was hollow, empty, and menacing. I fancied that he belonged to a different time.

My first rational thought, as I attempted to gain mental control of this situation, was simply that a hiker or someone had come down the ridge. I started to call out in some friendly way to him, to try and coax a simple friendly reaction in exchange, to banish all this fear- but the words wouldn't come. I was frozen, my spine shivering. As I looked closer at him, I began to feel some kind of menace in his stillness and his gaze. His eyes were pushing deep through me.

Then I realized he was naked. His skin was the color of the forest floor. At that moment, I thought a bird had landed on him because something large and brown reared up on his left shoulder. I felt dizzy with horror as I realized it was a fleshy, multi-legged thing, like some huge insect, crouching there on his body. His chest moved, and I realized that another one of these things was clinging to the front of his body.

I was overwhelmed with panic and I ran- I ran without even thinking about it. My instincts took over; adrenaline flooded me; and the world became very quiet and withdrawn. I saw the trees going by my face as I moved, and everything seemed strangely slow-moving. At some point in my panicked dash through the forest; I dropped the strange cup, but I don't know where.

I know that I was out there for at least a week before I was found. I know that you think I'm crazy, but as your fellow clinician and colleague, I can assure you and Dr. Gedney that I am as rational now as I always was. I chose to come here, to speak to you, to help you understand why it is very important that the state government- or someone- look carefully into this archaeological dig-site, and the caves near it. At your instruction, I have written this account of all the events that led me here to help you understand.

If we are intellectually honest men and women, we have to go where evidence leads. I'm not saying I have overpowering evidence in this case; or at least none that I can show you at this moment, but I know what I saw. I have another person- another educated person, a person of science- who claims to have seen the same things. There can surely be no harm in simply looking. We are all persons of learning, devoted to finding the truth. Do we not trust one another?

* * *

THE DAUGHTER OF BEL-TRABOL:

A Theory about a Curious Nursery Rhyme and its Relationship to Historical Witchcraft in Lancashire

Copyright 2006 by Susan Treadway, M.A.
Used with permission

* * *

"Ugly Lull Grinlee
Came of a witch's belly
A lame gal born of sin

Ugly Lull Grinlee
Smil'd all crookedly
Quite a simpleton

Ugly Lull Grinlee
Always quite lonely
Never had a friend

Ugly Lull Grinlee
Had to cry daily
For (her) mother's sin

Ugly Lull Grinlee
Took sick and happily
Was ne'er seen again"

-Child's Nursery Rhyme, circa 1800 from the Lancashire Historical Review (Vol. 21, 1974)

* * *

I.

James Anders-Myers, in his book "Martha Whitcroft: The Witch of Chimney Rock," talks about a sensational case of witchcraft in old Lancashire that took place in the late 17th century. With the current surge of interest, largely motivated by modern neo-pagan subculture in the more celebrated case of the Pendle Witches who were tried at the Lancaster Assizes on 18–19 August 1612, the story of Martha Whitcroft and her friends is often missed.

Following Anders-Myers, it seems that in 1670, A farm girl from outside the town of Clitheroe named Martha Whitcroft along with Mary Leadle, Jonet Hart, and Hilda Grenlea got up to some devilish business in the ruins of a seventh century abbey called Chimney Rock by the locals.

Chimney Rock was by that point mostly a pile of rocks, hidden away in a dense growth called Piked Acre wood and under a nearby rise called Worsaw hill, with a Roman road running alongside it which can still be seen and walked by tourists today. Another recording of the story claimed the misdeeds of the girls took place in Helliwell wood near a stream called Warth Beck, also outside of Clitheroe, but on the other side of the famed Pendle Hill which had gained a reputation for local witchcraft due to the trials some 60 years before.

The case appears straightforward: the girls had an orgy with the devil, and all but one of them got hanged for it after lengthy confessions. The lucky girl that escaped the noose did so only because she was pregnant- and miserably out of luck as she was, Hilda Grenlea died in childbirth with her family wanting nothing to do with her daughter, widely considered to be the devil's own child.

Hilda's sister apparently showed good Christian compassion and opted to raise the child, but she had to move to a nearby hamlet to do it as the people of Clitheroe wouldn't have the baby nearby for any reason. Of course, the countryside being quite connected, and with the tendency of rumors to fly far and wide, even the people in nearby areas had heard of the scandal, and wanted little to do with the infant girl or the girl's aunt.

The girl grew up to be an ugly duckling and coupled with the scorn of local adults and children, her reputation for being a daughter of the "evil one" was all but sealed. Her father was, based on the confessions given by her mother, a cottar from Sabden whom she "met on the white slacks". But the

"Martha Whitcroft, along with Mary Leadle, Jonet Hart, and Hilda Grenlea got up to some devilish business in the ruins of a seventh century abbey, called Chimney Rock by the locals."

scandal and the legend was set early and was unshakeable. The daughter was also quite sickly. Dr. Harold Whitby, in the Lancashire Historical Review, did a collection of nursery rhymes or play-songs for children in the 19th century, and one of them, given above, mentions a lonely, ugly girl named "Lull Grinlee".

I am of the opinion there is a high likelihood that this nursery rhyme is about the daughter of Hilda Grenlea- "Grinlee" and the surname Grenlea (probably derived from 'Green Lea' or "Green leaf/leaves") sound exactly alike, and the memory of local lore that gives rise to nursery rhymes is often framed in such ways. The rhyme was collected from an informant in Barrowford also in the shadow of Pendle hill.

Following along with my theory, which I admit is a theory, I would venture that the daughter of Hilda, whose name is never given in any source, was called "Lull". It's interesting that "Lullan" is a name given to a female fairy by English Folklorist and Historian Katherine Briggs in her celebrated books "The Encyclopedia of Fairies" and "The Vanishing People".

The nursery rhyme seems to indicate that the little girl took sick for a final time; perhaps buried somewhere in private by her long suffering aunt. But I would like to suggest that perhaps something else happened. What I have to suggest can stretch the boundaries of credulity, but please bear with me.

II.

It all started when I read the surviving excerpts from the confession of Mary Leadle, one of the Chimney Rock witches, and given by Anders-Myers. There isn't much from her confession that survived due to damage from a church fire that happened 75 years after her trial. In the partial confession, she admits that the "Devil" joined them in carnal union after a prayer was said to a "yellow rock" that was apparently shaped like a man's head and possibly marked with circles and other shapes. She said two other things-that two biblical psalms were used to make the devil appear and depart, and that his name (given to them by him) was "Beltrabul" or "Belthrabul".

My first thought was that this name was another one of those inscrutable and mysterious local devil-names, such as "Christsonday" (a name for the devil given by a rural healer, and recorded most recently by Margaret Murray) and the like.

But when I looked into the history of the Chimney Rock abbey and of the history of that region of Britain, I discovered that before the Briganti Celts were established as the dominant population a tribe of native Britons called the "Traboli" inhabited the area. They are the same people whose stone age predecessors may have put up the burial mounds on top of Pendle Hill.

With close archaeological ties to Mann and Wales, the Traboli certainly had a native tribal or toutal God that might have been assimilated with the coming of the later peoples into what we consider the Welsh/Brythonic "pantheon". These historical assimilations of the gods of native people with incoming cultural drifts is a well-known phenomenon. It is well known that a prominent Welsh Father God was called (variably) Bel or Beli. It may stretch the imagination, but when I considered the name "Beltrabul" for a while I thought "Bel of the Traboli"?

I admit that this may be a case of intuition seeing something that isn't there, but it inspired me to look further. The God Bel and the Traboli people are well known to historians. To put the two names together isn't as big a stretch as some might think though it must forever remain theoretical.

III.

The Abbey of Chimney Rock, now just a pile of rocks and ruins in the present day, was built after a recorded tussle with the local pagans. The monks who built it recorded the strife very briefly and used the rest of their chronicle to record the extravagant costs of maintaining so isolated a monastery and the tedium of keeping the offices of the hours. The record of the abbey is one of the manuscripts kept at an archive in the Oratory Church of St Aloysius Gonzaga in Oxford.

The monks do say that the local pagans, who were slow in converting, held dear to their idols and vain superstitions- even going as far as to occasionally offer their children to carved images. The people that these monks were talking about were related to the Brigantes; but in this area, they were also likely descendants of the Traboli.

Historians like to make comparisons between this mention of child sacrifice and the worship of Crom in Ireland- The stone idol Crom Cruaich, who at Moy Slecht, was reportedly offered children in exchange for "corn and fair weather".

The word "idol" kept coming up and when coupled with one more historical fact given by the monks, the fact that the monks buried the idols of the newly converted locals below the site of the abbey after breaking them up, I had another moment of insight that certainly makes my thesis here forever isolated from mainstream academia.

We should consider the possibility, however distant it might be, that the "yellow rock" mentioned in the witch trial which might have been shaped like a man's head, was actually a piece of a pagan idol that Martha and her friends had found at the ruins of Chimney Rock. I can appreciate how fantastical it may sound, but two pretty amazing coincidences seemed to be occurring: the name Beltrabul and the confession about the prayers to the idol-rock. The question that remained was again: was I seeing a shape where there was only a shadow? Stone age "cup and ring" marks are found on stones all over the British Isles; Mary Leadle said their rock had "circles and marks" on it.

IV.

So where would these girls have gotten the name "Beltrabul" from? They say they got it from the devil himself; but could they have gotten it from elsewhere? For a moment, let's say that I'm right about the origin of the name "Beltrabul" being "Bel of the Traboli"- there is no mention of it in any recorded folklore. The name only appears in the transcripts of this witch trial. Could there have been a thousand-year long tradition of people keeping this God's name alive or secret, and the girls heard about it from some local source? That would be too much to ask for- and impossible to prove.

Some have said that "Beltrabul" was just the recorder's misspelling of "Beelzebul"- or that the recorder misspelled it on purpose not wanting to write out the Devil's name. I personally like my theory better, but I admit that this is a good point to ponder.

But another point emerges that led me to my final conclusion which tied together several of these threads. Reginald Pitt, in the book "An Archaeological History of Lancashire, with a Study of Folklore, Superstition, and Legendry" mentions that two accused Witches in the mid 1700's who lived on the side of a stretch of forest called Bollard wood near the village of White Hough (again right below Pendle hill) asked a female demon named "Nan Lullan" to show them the future and in exchange, offered to give the demoness an infant.

Nan Lullan was experienced by these witches as female- an unusual thing for a "demon" to be because demonologists from that period and after it had no end of a time collecting endless catalogues of demonic names and one of the more "occult famed" catalogues- the Dictionairre Infernal- only lists one female demon out of the hundreds: Glasyabolus. That same demoness appears in the Goetia as a lone female demonic specimen.

Eighty years after Ugly Lull Grinlee 'got sick and sadly wasn't seen again', witches were asking a female demon or a female fairy named "Nan Lullan" for occult advice and considering giving, possibly sacrificing, a baby to her. This baby sacrifice could of course be the typical witch-hunt and witch trial related hysteria, but is it yet another simple coincidence that the Traboli people, again, living in that area in ancient times, were accused of the same, as an act of worship to their Idols?

Is it coincidence that Martha Whitcroft and her friends were worshipping a devil called "Beltrabul" on the exact geographic spot where monks record that they had buried broken idols from the Traboli/Briganti people; and that one of Martha's co-conspirators admitted that they had a "yellowish rock shaped like a man's head" which was prayed to bring forth their guest of honor?

My enjoyable romp through speculation ends with my theory that "Nan Lullan" might have been a fairy or demon, or possibly an eighty-year-old woman that local witches or peasants held in great reverence as being the daughter of the devil, or an old pagan god. Maybe the little girl Lull Grinlee- if that was her name- didn't die from her sickness, but survived to a ripe old age as a hermit in the woods in the area around Pendle hill. 'Nan Lullan' just means "Grandmother Lullan"- and old women were often called "Grandmother" as a polite honorific.

V.

My report doesn't end here. It ends with a dream I had.

Once again, and for the last time, maybe my imagination just got away with me, but this dream was quite disturbing in its intensity and its suggestion. I dreamed that Lull Grinlee was a monster, a real monster, living in a forest near Pendle Hill.

In my dream, she was at least eight feet tall with four short stubby legs, each ending in a foot that hat three terrible fleshy divisions. She shuffled when she walked. She had two long, skinny arms and a thick black body with equally-as-thick black fleshy tendrils hanging from her head like hair. It was a disturbing image that my subconscious mind decided to display to me to be certain. Her face was wide, withered on the right side, and the other side had a big staring eye; her nose was just some kind of hole in her face.

No, I don't normally dream such absurd-sounding things- but in the dream, after attempting- and failing- to run in terror, I saw a stone face behind the monster Lull Grinlee. I knew at that moment that she was, in fact, the daughter of the 'Man in the Yellow Rock': Bel-Trabol. I knew that he had impregnated Hilda Grenlea though invisibly and made all the Chimney Rock Witches feel great pleasure and worshipful desire for him. I realized that he wasn't a mortal being; that he was immortal in some fashion, and that he had probably been doing this to the native peoples who had found him here when they arrived from wherever their long migrations had taken them.

"In my dream, she was at least eight feet tall, with four short stubby legs, each ending in a foot that hat three terrible fleshy divisions. She shuffled when she walked."

When I consider the dream and the whole strange story, I always consider the idea that this thing or being- Beltrabol- was a local Spirit of the Land, something pre-human, part of the land long before mankind came about or around. In my dream, so draped as it was with fear, I also got the feeling that this thing didn't exactly have the bests interests of mankind in mind. The Traboli had worshipped him, made the special rocks in the area in his image, and offered him their children, possibly their firstborns.

Martha Whitcroft may indeed have found the remains of one of his idols there at Chimney Rock. It was just that kind of place. The Monks never stayed there long either (the Abbey was abandoned within 150 years of being built), and I don't imagine we should wonder why.

In my dream, I learned that "Ugly Lull Grinlee's" last sickness wasn't a sickness at all- it was more like a final transformation. She changed into something that was more like her father than her mother. In the dream, I saw her turn into a tree. I awoke thinking that she would live forever in those woods, and that when she stood still, from a distance, she looked like an old tree- and I gathered that she could sit still for a long time. It was a perfect disguise for such lonely, rural woods such as those.

Before you think my dream was high fantasy- I only have one more thing to say. In 1991, an American hiker named Jennifer Deury disappeared quite without a trace near the

vicinity of Pendle Hill and only her backpack was found in a local stretch of woods. Coincidence? One wonders.

* * *

"The Vicar's Well... was originally styled the "Leering Well" by the locals, presumably for the unsettling or malicious way the resident fairy lady of the well was said to gaze upon passers-by, especially if they were well formed or good-looking men."

THE LEERING WELL

* * *

"In the area of Gorse Hill, another example of fairy/human connubium relating to the "fatal fairy lover" motif (this time featuring a female fairy) is recorded twice. One mention is from Alfred of Cirencester in the mid-17th century, and the other is from the fieldwork of John Adwell, whose account appeared in the 1954 "Folk-Lore: A Quarterly Review of Myth, Tradition, Institution, & Custom."

The Vicar's Well (now situated on private property at the time of this writing) was originally styled the "Leering Well" by the locals, presumably for the unsettling or malicious way the resident fairy lady of the well was said to gaze upon passers-by especially if they were well formed or good-looking men.

Alfred of Cirencester gives a detail suggesting that the "Leering Well" was so named after a "reverence of great antiquity" devoted to an obscure (and elsewhere unattested) female saint named Lera to whom the well was held sacred. Historians are of one mind in suggesting that "Saint Lera" was not a historical figure connected to the Church or early Christianity in Britain, but likely a local spirit or native goddess-type character, many of whom prefigure later fairy legends and whose presence had been attached in folk-memory to the well. A separate tradition attaches the well to Saint Anne.

The passage of time had not diminished Lera's activities around Gorse Hill; Adwell gives a vibrant account from local informants in 1951 regarding the danger of traveling alone or in the evening on the road that ran below the well. Youthful or handsome men traveling by themselves might be entranced and abducted by the fairy-lady, who thought nothing of keeping them for several days or weeks though the men were unaware of the passage of time while in her company. And although Lera didn't seem kill her paramours, every man who encountered her pined for her until the end of his days and was unable to free himself of desire for her. This led to some of them ending their own lives in despair. One such man is said to have drowned himself in the well.

The Leering Well was given the name "Vicar's Well" in the 1890's after a local minister purchased the land containing the well and had it sealed for fear that his children might fall into it while playing.

Lera's unsettling gaze and irresistible beauty were both mentioned by Adwell's informants; Alfred of Cirencester's passage from three and a half centuries earlier mentions the same. This is an astounding and detailed example of the persistence of local traditions..."

-Ruth Lyndell Teague, "Wiltshire Folklore and Legends."

***

"Around its dark wood frame were carved the faces of the damned, calling out- and it was crowned by a horned face of terrible majesty."

THE MAN IN THE MIRROR

* * *

Denise glanced up from her book and notes and down again. Carefully she sounded out the words, looking up as much as her memory allowed, and staring with some fear and excitement at her deeply shadowed reflection in the great mirror before her which was illumined only by candlelight.

Spells were not easy to cast. It seemed so hard to "get her mind right", to block out the lights and sounds of television, and to ignore the growl of passing cars outside. When she sat down at night in her bedroom, it seemed more like an afterthought not a mighty work of sorcery.

That all changed when her great aunt Esther died. Before the estate sale, the old lawyer handling the deal allowed Denise and her mother to come and have their pick of what they wanted from Esther's massive, crumbling manor. When Denise saw the mirror, she knew she had to have it. How Esther could have obtained something like this, she never could figure out. She heard that her aunt's first husband had traveled a lot in India and Central Asia, but this mirror challenged everything she had imagined about those exotic places.

Around its dark wood frame were carved the faces of the damned, calling out- and it was crowned by a horned face of terrible majesty; her secret interest in the occult came to life when she locked eyes with the horned face. It was "Him", the Great Entity described on all those websites devoted to traditional witchcraft and the "left-hand path" discussion groups that she spent so much time on.

When she saw herself in the mirror the first time, it was as though the room she was in- full of junk and cloth-covered furniture- was no longer there; for one instant, it seemed that she stood in darkness perhaps in a deep cave with a dim, red glow framing her hair and face. It was her phone beeping to alert her to a text message that made her refocus her eyes and see the room in the mirror just as it was around her.

Her mother was less than pleased at her choice, but she brought the old mirror home. Even the old lawyer protested a bit- he said he thought the mirror was very old and could be worth quite a penny. Denise didn't care. When she practiced her trance-work or her banishing rituals before the mirror, she felt different; she felt like she was actually performing a great and mystical art, a sorceress from long ago, before her shrine of magical working. And the horned man gazing down on her- the sight of him invoked all of the mysteries of the occult and forbidden.

And now, on this night, deep in the hidden season of the White Solstice, she faced the mirror again, chanting the words of the ritual from her book. The words were too difficult and long to commit to memory so she struggled by candlelight to read them off the paper and to say them while facing into the dark ocean of the mirror's ghostly surface, made weirdly luminous by the dots of candlelight.

She slipped up and mispronounced the last word of the refrain to her summoning incantation. She swiftly re-spoke, correcting herself- or at least, making it as correct as she thought it should be based on the Classical Greek pronunciation website she had found earlier that morning. She said it again, and again, and discovered that she liked the sound of it; it was almost like a drumbeat in her head.

She resolved to concentrate hard and keep reading this as many times as she needed to. She began to raise her voice a bit- not too loud lest she disturb her mother who was asleep downstairs directly below her- and started to enjoy what she was doing. It was as though a switch had gone off in her head; the pronunciation became effortless, and her own voice began to speak as though it were speaking on its own.

Time passed, but Denise didn't know how much. She stopped suddenly, disquieted by a feeling or an awareness she couldn't quite place- before she realized the drone of cars outside had stopped. It was deadly quiet and still in her bedroom- more so than she had ever experienced. There was no sound, no droplet of sound, except the hiss of the candles which now seemed very loud like a cat's hiss. Even the streetlights outside seemed to be gone; her blinds were no longer softly glowing. She couldn't hear the central heating in the house mumbling as it always did.

She got up and walked to the windows, bent one of the blinds, and peaked outside. It was like black ink had been poured over her windowpanes; she saw nothing but her own reflected eyes, now full of fear, looking back at her.

She then noticed that the light in the room was gradually changing- from the golden hue cast by the candles to a soft, deep red. The candle flames were slowly turning red! In thoughtless panic, Denise darted for her bedroom door, but she never made it; she lost consciousness and crashed down to the carpet halfway to her escape.

Balkylix, The Man in the Mirror, and the daimonic servitors that he had collected about himself for 3000 mortal years surged out of the mirror and into the four-dimensional world again, finally free of their trance-like imprisonment in the fifth dimensional probability plane behind the dark glass of the Mirror of Laertes.

The mortal tetraspace was cold; without the imaginary substance behind the glass to give forms to their minds, all they could do was exist in the room dimly aware of enclosing matter but with no means to grasp it or apprehend it beyond shadows. Balkylix was more powerful than the twisted and hopeless beings he had attracted and shaped to his will. He saw more; he felt more. As soon as he could penetrate the eyes of the girl asleep on the floor, he could transfer his will into her brain and enjoy the feeling of nerve endings again. Time had meaning here.

It had been ages since Alexander's men had carried his reliquary with them to the silk-draped courts of Sogdiana and thence to the majestic mountains of Bactria where he, Balkylix, the Wolf of Secrets and the Obsidian Scarab of Hidden Things, gave oracles to the daughters and sons of conquered Kings. It had been ages since the great fire that destroyed his sacred receptacle, and the blasphemy that had banished him to lurk resentfully in the dark forests bereft of form... and centuries since Laertes the Magian had imprisoned him in the abyss of glass.

Slowly, Denise stood up. When he saw his reflection in the mirror for the first time, so youthful, with long dark hair and warm white skin, Balkylix understood how the human girl had disrupted Laertes' Conjuration of Dodecahedral Entrapment. It had nothing to do with the Ancient Greek conjuration she had chanted (and to which her pronunciation was completely dreadful) and everything to do with the desire that burned inside her heart and filled her eyes. She wanted so much more than this world; the mirror had tried to pull the dark desire out of her and take it into itself.

But the mirror was full already, Balkylix mused with inconceivable delight. The hateful crystalline force summoned by that self-righteous fool Laertes had cracked and vanished when it was over-taxed. It had already begun to grow weak through the fateful circular whirling of the planets and stars for countless rotations of the sky.

Denise picked up the book that she had secretly ordered from online, and Balkylix looked at the cover; it read "The Goetia of Pymander: A Postmodern Approach to Scrying, Invoking, and Conjuring Spirits." Denise tossed it aside with a small chuckle of amusement.

Balkylix spoke in his new voice for the first time to the unseen host of twisted-necked beings drifting in the room, seeking warmth for themselves- the warmth that they had been denied since their executions by hanging centuries ago.

"My mother lies downstairs" Denise said. "She is foolish, weak, and asleep. Colonize her. We will cast her off when we find someone more suitable." Balkylix loved the feeling of speaking a new language. Denise's brain and vocal cords moved to express his will so easily and the sounds she made- such strange sounds!

The door of Denise's room swung open as though invisible hands had yanked it with great force. All at once, odd sounds surged over Balkylix's new ears: someone leaned on a car horn outside, and the non-stop wail of sirens moaned in the background. Denise picked up a large perfume bottle from the table at the side of her bed and smashed the Mirror of Laertes into countless sharp pieces. She walked to her window and tore the blinds away.

Balkylix stared eagerly at the countless lights of the enormous buildings protruding from downtown miles away and looked up in wonder as the blinking light of an airplane on its approach to land passed overhead, rumbling in the dark clouds. Denise smiled. It was a brave new world, indeed.

***

THE WITCH WHO BLIGHTED LEEKLEY

This story is inspired by actual events that occurred in the English Countryside, in the ruined churchyard near Clophill, in 1963.

* * *

They say my great, great, great grandmother was a witch. I say "great, great, great" because I've lost count of the generations; the records get spotty sometimes. Let's just say it was a hell of a long time ago.

Back in this grandmother's living days, being a single mother was unheard of, and yet she lived quite single and alone with her infant twin daughters in a cottage on the distant edge of Leekley. The fact that this great grandmother of mine was a feisty, red-haired beauty didn't help her reputation any. There's no baptism record, but I know that her name was Azariah. She lived in the cottage with her two little girls, and according to one source, kept various fowls, one black billy, and two grey nans.

They said she was a witch and looking back at the stories that have come down to me and considering what I now know, I'd say they were definitely right. Most of the time, being called a "witch" just meant you were unpopular with the local church wives, or that you had landed in bed with one of their husbands. Turns out, my grandmother had done that, too.

But unlike the other women that the local rich man farmer Barclay used and ruined, my grandmother knew a thing or two about what really hurt a man of the land's business: it is said that she buried a dead toad under one of his birch trees- and after that, his hens began laying stones instead of eggs. He had a lot of hens. That was a lot of stones.

Most people today find this to be an amusing, harmless revenge. But back then, it was actually quite a dangerous thing because it led to accusations that could lead to a gallows pole. William Barclay, accompanied by his very jealous wife, led the mob that came to my grandmother's cottage to round her up for the local magistrate.

They never managed to find her on their own, though. They kicked her door in only to find her two toddler daughters bundled up in the corner sleeping soundly, and no sign of my grandmother. They knew she was in the cottage, because they had seen her go in before they surrounded the place and beat her door in. They immediately looked in the fireplace and up the chimney, thinking she had hid there, but there was no sign of her. At this point, the clear facts were apparent to the mob: she wasn't in the chimney because she had flown up it and away.

The wife of Farmer William wasn't going to let something as silly as flying powers ruin her revenge, however. She seized one of the young daughters of my grandmother and ran outside with her, yelling to the sky and the trees that the little girl would come to harm if the mother didn't turn herself over to God and man- and guess what? It worked. That night, my grandmother walked into the village and turned herself in.

Yeah, it was pretty horrid to threaten an innocent little girl, just to catch her mother- but it happened. What exactly she threatened to do to her, I never found out; no one ever mentioned it. But it was enough.

From what I've come to understand by reading up on local folklore, one of the ways people used to make evil fairies and spirits return human children they had stolen was by threatening the "changeling" child that the fairies left behind; sometimes, they even burned what looked to everyone like an innocent human baby. Sometimes, it worked. Sinister, mind-twisting beings would creep out of the darkness on the other side of the village hedge to return children, rescuing their offspring, leaving behind a crying human baby and partially insane parents. But sometimes, a child just died.

Either way, threatening a child to coerce the obedience of a supernatural being had a long precedent in those parts. And this time, as I said before, it worked. My grandmother went to trial and was sentenced rather quickly to swing. But it wasn't just about William Barclay's eggs or his unwilling entry into the gravel business. It wasn't about the former philandering minister's withered penis. It wasn't even about my grandmother's alleged rapist being crushed bodily in half by the gears of the mill by the river, or the way the bread produced from the flour made at that mill screamed with his voice when people bit into it. It was about a woman that wouldn't be humbled.

"They say my great, great, great grandmother was a witch."

As an interesting aside, at her trial my grandmother said a man taught her some things in the graveyard down the lane from her cottage deep in the spinney where the older village and church had been before everyone moved to be closer to the developing roads. The man was never named or found, but he seems to have had a fascination with graves and the dead. She was taught that digging up bones and arranging them in a special way caused a "path" to open; a path for dead souls to come back into the world and enter the womb of a fertile woman who had just been (or was just being) impregnated. Maybe her graveyard man was the Devil himself; the popular opinion at the time said that he surely was.

Well, anyway, folktales aside, they hanged her. Her last words to the minister were "silence, you." Her last words to the people gathered to watch her die were "red milk."

The day after that, farmers and people milking cows in Leekley got a nasty surprise in the early morning: blood was all that came from the udders of their cows. No cow in Leekley ever gave milk again, only blood. William Barclay, whose entire stock of cows and chickens was now useless, went broke. He drank himself to death, and his wife, a bitter lady till the end, died in a workhouse, very ugly and broken, years later.

As for the twin daughters of the witch who blighted Leekley, well, one of them died of a fever very soon after my grandmother's hanging. The surviving daughter, she vanishes from history, taken by some unknown family far away, perhaps distant relatives. But her mother, my grandmother, was buried near a crossroads a mile away where unbaptised children and suicides got buried. She wasn't fit for holy ground.

About ten years after this all happened, a grave got robbed- the grave of the little daughter of my grandmother. Somebody took her little skull and the bones of her left hand, leaving the other bones exposed. And that was just the start of the trouble. Disaster after disaster started happening after that, to every person who was involved with the lynch-mob that came for my grandmother. One by one, the nastiest of things happened: crazed horse accidents, lethal fevers, heart attacks, and the like.

...Anyway, folktales aside, they hanged her. Her last words to the minister were "silence, you." Her last words to the people gathered to watch her die were "red milk."

Nor were their families spared; children died too. Investigators got a real tip-off one day when a young maid from a village up the road was accused of witchcraft and caved in under questioning herself. The Man in Black, the Bone Man, (she said) was getting revenge. His lover, Azariah the Leekley Witch, was murdered, and he wanted revenge.

She admitted that she helped him to rob the grave of the little girl. Why? Because the Spirit of the Leekley Witch could only be summoned by threatening her daughter- in this case, by threatening to smash her daughter's skull and hand to dust. If you carried the skull and hand and threatened to do that down at the crossroads, the vengeful spirit of that red-haired woman would do what you asked. A sinister yet effective charm.

For her testimony and her confession and (I'm sure very sincere) repentance, this maid was released. She, at least, didn't have to hang. But the investigators furiously hunted the man in Black, the Bone Man, who was bringing havoc down on the village and the area. They never found him, and the remains of the families who were involved in the Leekley Witch incident fled the town. There isn't any record of what became of them in other places, but I wouldn't personally wager a bucket of piss about whether or not they came to good ends.

I know that Leekley didn't come to any good end. It was swallowed by the forest and is nothing but a forest now. A forest that everyone swears is haunted, and that you sometimes find ruined stone walls in. I don't think it was much of a loss. Old Leekley is still just a stretch of woods. The modern village is a little bit more to the east.

* * *

Here's where it gets strange, but hear me out.

I got a visit, about a month ago, from a gentleman who refused to come inside my house. He wanted to talk outside. He always dressed all in black, and he visited me at dusk for about seven days in a row, always leaving before the cock crowed the next dawn. By all good sense and reason, I should have been afraid of him- he was a terrible and wondrous sight to behold. I can't call him handsome, but his dark features were still compelling to look at. My first thought upon seeing him was that I was about to be murdered, but he had a surprising way of making me at ease around him.

He knew a lot about my grandmother, and told me something that I'd never heard before. He said that before she went to turn herself in to the local magistrate, she had told him that she'd come back with the sun in her hand.

I asked him how he knew that, and he told me that he *was* the Bone Man. I told him that the Bone Man would have to be dead for many generations now, and he told me that no one who understood the *Road of the Red Bones* had to die for good. He then told me a very interesting tale.

Apparently, the two graveyards in old Leekley were both built on old pagan temples; one temple to some thunder god, a divine strongman who carried a big mallet and a wheel, and other to the gods of the underworld who were always in the company of black snakes and black roosters. The dead, I was told, "went down below" at one cemetery, but came back through another. When the cock crowed, the King Below called the dead away; they couldn't resist the cock's crow. But when the days were right, the sky parted, and the dead could come back if the graveyard road was made clear.

It was done by opening a grave, taking all the bones out, making a big circle with them, and placing the skull in the center. Then a big wheel with four spokes had to be painted in red on a flat piece of stone nearby, a stone that pointed to heaven. Apparently, the ruined stone church wall worked just fine for this, because its steeple pointed to heaven, or it had once. Then when the name of the dead person was intoned, a man studded a woman in the circle- and as long as the bones were of a female relative, the spirit could "leap" into the womb of the woman being impregnated and gain for itself a new life-house.

When the person came out as a newborn baby, they didn't really remember their previous life, but a member of the Bone Society had a way of rekindling those memories. The Man in Black said that he had died and been back down the bone road dozens of times around the area of Leekley. He remembered dozens of lives wherein he had done this operation for many others like himself- and so it went. There was more than one of him, and they kept to themselves quite in secret.

I was a little shocked and mystified by his story, but something about the way he talked and the way he looked just told me that he wasn't lying. He then offered me a little bottle asking me to drink what was inside. When I asked what it was, he said it was a means of remembering.

I then asked him if I was one of his old clients, and he laughed and said that I was; he said I was his very favorite client whom he missed very much. He told me that when I was born, I was yellow- I had jaundice, but in my left hand I was holding a clot of bright yellow pus or something just as grotesque; the midwife had even remarked (never having heard our local stories of witches), "Oh look! The little girl's got the sun in her hand!"

I drank the potion. I felt sick and then fell asleep.

When I woke up, the first thing I did was go down with my beloved Man in Black to the old churchyard in the tangled woods to a great tree whose secret hollow held the bones of my beloved daughter Betsey- hidden there by the Man in Black all this time. I was here again because of her bones. She will be here again, and my long-lost Charisa will be soon, too, for my lover and I are as nobles in the Kingdom of Bones. A love like ours is very unique. To stand between us and our love is to stand in Hell's way, a thing many of the unhappy and untimely dead have learned to their detriment.

"It was done by opening a grave, taking all the bones out, and making a big circle with them, and placing the skull in the center."

Through the dense undergrowth and the layers of filth and all-consuming time, I could see the land as it used to be. It was my great pleasure to spit on what was left of the grave of William Barclay. I would have spit on his wife's grave, but she was put into an unmarked mass grave somewhere, and forgotten. And *that* is a happy ending.

***

THE TALE OF THORKELL AND THE TROLL

* * *

I. How Thorkell became an Outlaw

Thorkell, son of Olvir, grandson of Hormstein Long-Leg, was in his thirty-fifth year when he was declared an outlaw by the local assembly of free men in Langidal. Standing there in the *domhringur*, the circle of judgment, the sentence of lesser outlawry was passed on him.

Some would say that Thorkell was lucky; he had killed Ivar, son of Hogni, whose family was the wealthiest in the region. Thorkell could not afford the man-price for Ivar, but the assembly accepted half of his herd of sheep as a fine and expelled him from the land for three years. Cooler heads prevailed at the assembly because no one desired a new blood feud which could spill over into further killing. It also happened that the assembly leader, Thorgest, was a friend of Thorkell's father from years before, and through some means, he worked out leniency.

Even with his life and some wealth spared, Thorkell was devastated, for he knew that the judgment was a death sentence on his two sons, who were not yet men. Even though the law allowed Thorkell to put aside the rest of his wealth to support his family in his absence, he knew that Hogni's men would find a way to kill his sons. He knew they would take his sheep and burn his home; and he could not be there to stop it.

Thorkell had come to Langidal from the mainland in his twenty-fifth year and married Elsa, the daughter of Hjalti. After eight years of adventure and raiding southern lands, he had become weary of constant voyages and fighting and weary of the constant feuding at his home overlooking Hardangerfjord. He had sailed across the Northern Ocean to find a calmer life.

His marriage and the birth of his twin sons was a further sign to Thorkell that the Gods favored his decision, but after three years, hard winters had thinned his herd and his other fortunes. His sons grew to their tenth years, but his wealth did not grow and want began to stalk his family. While drowning his sorrows in ale at the Winter Nights assembly, he found himself in angry, drunken words with Ivar in a fight over a slave girl.

Thorkell held no grudges, but Ivar was rash and young. A month later, Ivar picked a fight with Thorkell while he was rounding up sheep on the Blanda heath, and in a heated struggle, Thorkell crushed Ivar's skull with a stone.

Thorkell was given one month to prepare for his departure. By law, he could stay at three homes or farmsteads, all of which had to be on his way to the coast, and to a ship that he would arrange to take him away. If he should leave any of these three farms, or the narrow roads between them, he could be killed on sight. If he lingered too long without sailing away, he could be attacked and killed. Taking his family away from their farm was not possible; their farm was all they had and nothing remained for him on the mainland. Hjalti, his father-in-law, was very old and had no sons to protect his daughter or his grandsons.

Thus, his family's safety during his three-year absence fell to his close friend Vestein, son of Orm. Vestein was also from the mainland and had his own problems and distractions. Thorkell found himself in a raging sorrow that he could not escape which only got stronger as he came to his final stopping-place, the last farm at which he would take refuge before he boarded a boat the next morning for points unknown.

Vestein had traveled with him, and if it were not for his friend's counsel and assurances, Thorkell would certainly have remained at his home and died there. Leaving was the hardest thing he had ever done. Riding together through a very cold night, Thorkell and Vestein arrived at Garmund's farm.

II. Garmund's Farm

"Thorkell the sheep herder... even after all this time, it's still hard to believe."

Vestein drained his horn of ale and looked around the firelit inside of Garmund's lodge-house, looking for the girl who was carrying the pitcher among the laughing guests. Several children were darting barefooted around the knees of the men and women.

Thorkell answered without looking up. "I'm a husband and a father now, and when there isn't ice in your beard and in your arse, sheep are a fine enough living."

Vestein grinned as the slender girl refilled his horn. "A husband and a father? You don't miss the sailing and splashing through the foam and taking other people's money?"

Thorkell finally looked up. "That life is piss and wind. The 'glory gold' never lasts. Sheep make more sheep, and if you keep 'em fat and safe, and get a good market day, that's months of supplies and wood. Besides, you grow to like a land and get to know a place. Last I heard, you were still laying girls in ports and camps, girls whose names you don't even remember. When you find a good woman, you'll want to settle down on a farm somewhere, too."

Vestein shook his head. "You know; they still tell stories about you back home. 'Thorkell the reaver' they call you, and they say the boats that go raiding now never have the luck they had when you were on them. You were young, but you inspired boys to glory. Now you're an old man watching sheep out here in the middle of the ocean."

Thorkell didn't answer. Vestein pressed him. "Hey old man did you hear me? They still tell stories about you back on the mainland."

Thorkell drained his horn. "They do? Hey... what about that girl from Bergholm... the one with the long red hair that we met that time- does she still tell stories about me?"

"Who, Gyda? Yeah, she tells stories about you. She says you must like sheep more than women; she says you fell asleep while rutting her that night."

Thorkell narrowed his eyes while Vestein laughed at his reaction. "She said that?"

"Is it true?"

"Yes, but that had nothing to do with her. I was just tired."

Vestein laughed harder. "More ale for my friend!" he called to the serving girl just as the doors to the lodge opened and three men entered, trailing a gust of wind.

Vestein craned his neck to get a look at them, but Thorkell already knew them. "That's Herjolf. His boat takes me away tomorrow." His looks darkened.

Vestein looked at Thorkell and softened his voice. "You're coming back in just three winters. Bersi and Anlaf and I won't let any of Hogni's men within five miles of your farm. You have my oath on that."

Thorkell couldn't meet his eyes. "I think you mean what you say, but Bersi is a drunk, and Anlaf will be outlawed before long. You travel all the time, and you're landless now. Your heart's good, but I don't know that anyone can watch over my wife and my sons the way they need."

"Thorgest won't let anything happen."

"Thorgest can't stop anything. He's fallen behind since his brother died, and Hogni and his kin are the power now. Everything is coming to ruin for those I love the most. I cannot get on that ship tomorrow."

Vestein leaned in closer. "We were followed all the way to Flosi's farm. Rhorvald and Runolf are probably camped outside right now, up on the rocks, hoping that you step too far away from this house to take a piss so that they can kill you. There's no going back now. I told you, I'm going to take care of your wife and boys- I'll die to protect them if the Allfather decides it so."

Thorkell leaned back and closed his eyes. Death would have been preferable to this punishment.

III. Mixed Company

The ale had finally begun to take affect and Thorkell found himself dazed staring at the wall as Vestein told stories about the newly-discovered lands further west. Thorkell was unable to escape his memories of his sobbing wife. He could still feel her tears on his hands. He kept seeing the faces of his sons trying hard to act brave for him as he laid swords in their hands, telling them that they were men now.

He snapped out of his daze when another cold air blast hit him- the door had opened again, and this time, a figure in a heavy hooded fur cloak entered. The door slammed shut and the people sitting near turned to look. Without fail, they all fell silent and looked at one another in surprise.

Vestein turned and looked for a long moment. He whipped his head toward Thorkell with alarm on his face. "Thor's hammer! I can't believe she has the gut to walk in here!"

The figure let the fur hood drop and indeed, it was a woman. It was impossible to say how old she was, but her tangled black hair was streaked grey in places. She had deep lines around her mouth. Her dark eyes were sharp and clear, and they swept back and forth around the large room that was suddenly much quieter.

"Who is this woman?" Thorkell asked with a lower voice to Vestein.

Vestein whispered back. "Rannveig. She's a witch, a sorceress who isn't allowed around the farms up here. She should have been killed a dozen times, but the godi Thorgrim won't let the local assembly just get rid of her."

Thorkell looked at the woman again. "A witch?"

"A gods-cursed seeress who brings death and ill-luck on the people that she lives near enough to. A year ago, at Moberg, I saw her sit on one of those high seats, make all sorts of howls and noises, and begin talking to what she said were 'spirits'. She made all kinds of predictions- not all of which made the company there very happy. She wasn't made welcome again."

"Why does Thorgrim protect her?"

"The figure let the fur hood drop and indeed, it was a woman. It was impossible to say how old she was, but her tangled black hair was streaked grey in places. She had deep lines around her mouth. Her dark eyes were sharp and clear..."

"Who knows? She probably has some spell on him. She isn't allowed near people so she lives by herself up on the rocks somewhere. Two of the men at Moberg that she said would die before the year was out *did die*. Their families accused her of bringing the bane down on them that led to their deaths. She's trouble, Thorkell."

Rannveig hadn't moved from the door since she entered. People began to mutter, and one man even stood up glaring at her. Rannveig met his gaze with an icy look.

From across the lodge-room, Garmund's wife, Alfhild, walked quickly towards Rannveig. "You are welcome here, Rannveig," she said in a voice that seemed loud in the hushed room. "As the woman of this house, I welcome you and offer you drink." She offered Rannveig a silver cup.

Rannveig's look softened and she gave a half smile and accepted it. The man who had stood slowly sat down, and the conversation in the room gradually grew louder.

From his seat, Garmund, the master of the farm, was watching intently. His wife turned her head and met his eyes not breaking her look until Garmund nodded once and went back to his guests.

"Did you see that?" Thorkell asked Vestein.

"Yes, I saw. I can only wonder what that witch has hanging over the heads of Garmund and Alfhild that would lead them to welcome her here. Thorkell, we should get out of here and get to our beds; this isn't a very good place to be now."

"I think you're shaming yourself being so afraid of a woman," Thorkell said. "I've seen a seeress make predictions before. I don't think they can make things happen the way you think they can. I think people just like to blame other people when bad things happen."

Vestein gave him a bewildered look. "Do you hear yourself? She's a witch! She doesn't just know people's fates; she gets spirits to do bad things to people. Either she willfully does it, or she can't control whatever evil follows her around. I don't want her near me in either case. So much for Garmund's hospitality!"

Thorkell took another cup of ale from the table. "I don't care about the witch. I have my own problems. I still don't think she can make people die. There were sorcerers and witches back on the mainland too, if you recall. My father didn't think they had all the power people said they did, either. Let's just drop it."

Vestein a sip from his horn, but didn't take his eyes off Rannveig. Suddenly he reached out and swatted Thorkell's arm.

"She's coming over here!" he whispered urgently.

Thorkell looked up. Surely enough, Rannveig was not only staring at him, she was walking up his side of the long table. He felt a moment of trepidation, but he calmed himself quickly. He didn't fear the woman, but he did find it hard to dismiss a lifetime of stories about the dangerous powers of witches.

Rannveig sat on the long bench only two body-spaces from Thorkell. For Vestein, that was too close. Summoning courage, he spoke up.

"I know that you have been made welcome here by the woman of the house, but we don't want the wind of you. Find another seat."

Rannveig took a sip from her cup and ignored Vestein. She spoke to Thorkell.

"You're Thorkell, Son of Olvir. I see that hard times have entangled you."

Thorkell looked at Rannveig. "Everyone in these parts knows my troubles, but my business is my own. I want nothing to do with you, woman. Leave us in peace."

"You're Thorkell, Son of Olvir, who is preparing to board a ship when the sun comes up. You fear what will happen to your sons when you are gone. And you are right to fear- if you go, they will not live to see their father return."

Thorkell's face went cold. His first impulse was to strike this woman, but he held back. Assaulting a guest who was made welcome by the lady of the hall would be breaking the peace required by Garmund's hospitality.

Vestein spoke before he could. "Woman, his sons will be looked after, and you aren't doing any good being here. Leave before we have to break the peace of this table."

Rannveig finally looked at Vestein. "Olvir's son already knows in his heart what you know in your head- that you can't always be there to watch over his family. And you won't be staying here much longer, anyway; you too will be forced to leave."

Vestein struggled not to let his jaw shake. "What? That's absurd. I wouldn't-"

"You will, because Hogni's sons won't leave you with a choice, and we both know you treasure your own life more than any other. I have come here to speak with Thorkell, not you."

The color drained out of Vestein's face.

Thorkell stood up. "That's enough," he said firmly. He towered over the seated witch, but she didn't move. She slowly looked up at him.

"Thorkell, I can help you. Your sons don't have to be abandoned to the wolves that circle them. If you have any share of wisdom in you, you will hear me out. I did not come here to trouble you or any other."

Thorkell smirked. "You came here to help me, a total stranger, out of the goodness of your heart? I can't believe that, and now, I have to rest before I board my ship."

Rannveig's hand shot out and seized Thorkell's arm as he moved away. "No, Thorkell, I didn't come here just to help you; I came here because I know that we can help each other. I need a service of you. If you do something for me, I can see that your outlawry is reversed."

Thorkell blinked once and stared at her. His heart began to pound.

"This is her idea of a joke, Thorkell. Leave the witch and let's go!" Vestein was insistent.

Thorkell couldn't move. The woman's gaze was paralyzing. He couldn't believe her, but what if she knew something?

"We can't talk about this in here," Rannveig said. "If you want to hear the rest of my offer then meet me outside when the moon is high at Garmund's cattle-pin."

Rannveig put her cup on the table. She looked across the room at Alfhild, who was watching, and nodded to her. Then she tied on her cloak and vanished back into the windy night.

IV. Loyalty to Kin

"You aren't going to speak to that witch. I won't let you. There's no telling what she's doing out there." Vestein was staring incredulously at Thorkell from across the table.

"Vestein, you're a good friend, but don't think to tell me what I can't do."

"Thorkell, stop being pig-headed! There's no chance of her reversing your outlawry! She probably wants to take blood from you or try to get you to kill someone that she hates in exchange for false promises. She knows you're desperate for a chance to stay here. Think this through! Let's just go to sleep now!"

Thorkell got up and walked out into the freezing night. The door hadn't even closed fully when Vestein threw it open and came running up behind him.

"Thorkell, have you ever considered that she's luring you out here so that Hogni's sons can get a shot at you? They could have paid her!"

Thorkell spun around. "You have helped me enough, Vestein. You have my thanks. Now, I will do what I feel I must. I'm a father who is about to lose his sons. I owe it to them and to my wife to give an ear to this woman. If Hogni's kin are hiding somewhere, let them come at me. I'm armed; fate will decide who wins. I'm not afraid of dying in a fight. But I am afraid of losing my family. You'd understand this if you had sons."

"I have loyalty to my kin, you don't have to remind me what it is!" Vestein yelled back at him.

"What kin you have left are a thousand miles from here and in no danger. When the sun is up tomorrow, my wife and sons will be like sheep left for the wolves. I'm going to talk to this woman. If she tells me nonsense, I'll laugh her off and go to bed. That's all I have to say. Wait for me by the fire inside."

Vestein shook his head and walked away.

V. Secret Knowledge

Rannveig was standing with her back to Thorkell as he approached. The stars were out with a full moon spilling pristine white light on the rugged landscape. Standing on the low hill near Garmund's cattle-pin, Thorkell could see for miles around. He could hear the sound of wind and water and smell the salt of the nearby ocean.

"How can you reverse my outlawry, woman?" Thorkell spoke to her back impatient to hear what she had to say.

"I can show you something- a secret- that will force Hogni's brother-in-law Sturla to revoke his decision to outlaw you. He will convince Hogni through bribery to call a new assembly, and he will vote in favor of overturning your outlawry. Thorgest, and all the other men who voted in your favor will be happy to do so again; as I recall, you were outlawed by only one vote to begin with."

Thorkell felt his heart sink. The woman was speaking nonsense.

"Are you mad, woman? There is nothing you could show me that would make Sturla do any such thing! And Hogni would never be swayed; I killed his youngest son. Speak sense to me, or I'll go back inside."

"Hogni hasn't just lost a son recently. You know as well as I that he lost a brother, too."

"Yes, his brother Hord got lost in the last ice storm. What of it?"

"His brother Hord wasn't lost to a storm. Sturla killed him."

Thorkell's head spun. "What?"

"Sturla and Hord got into a fight, and Sturla killed Hord. Hord slew Sturla's favorite slave, and in anger, Sturla slew Hord. Fearing what Hogni would do, Sturla buried the bodies on his own property. People assumed that Hord had been lost when the storm made the glacier wall collapse because Hord was taking the road through that valley the day before."

"How could you possibly know this? Did you witness it?"

"Hord told me himself."

"Wha-" Thorkell stopped before he could get the rest of his words out. Rannveig turned and met his eyes with her own. They seemed like dark lumps of coal in the moonlight.

Thorkell felt fear begin to crawl in his gut. "Hord... told you?"

"I can see the dead and speak to them," Rannveig said. "Hord found me and told me."

Thorkell swallowed hard and then shook his head. "This is nonsense. Whatever dreams or visions you claim to have are no evidence for your wild accusations. No one would believe a word you say, besides. You aren't welcome anywhere."

"It is precisely because people *do* believe my words that I have found myself to be unwelcome," Rannveig hissed. "But I can offer you more than my word and more than the words of a dead man. If you help me, I'll show you where the graves are. If you tell Sturla what you know, and threaten to reveal him to Hogni, he will help you, even though he will despise you. Hogni hates Sturla; he hates that his sister married him. Just finding these graves will be enough proof for Hogni; he would feud against Sturla, and he would kill him and burn his home to the ground."

"What you say may be true about Hogni, and all the rest, but I still don't know that you aren't making this up to get me to do… whatever it is you want me to do. You can't show me the graves beforehand because then I would have no reason to help you."

Rannveig walked forward and put out her hand to Thorkell.

"What do you want?" Thorkell asked, backing away a bit.

"Your hand," Rannveig said.

Thorkell forced his hand to stop shaking and put his palm in hers.

Rannveig closed her eyes for a moment. "There are a woman's tears on this hand. This same tear-stained hand put two swords of poor quality into the hands of two boys less than a fortnight ago. Those swords aren't fit to be wielded, but they are all you could get."

Thorkell pulled his hand back roughly. He was the only person, aside from his sons and his wife, who had been there for the gifting of those swords.

"Woman, you are wicked. You have no right to gain this knowledge of other people. It doesn't belong to you!"

Rannveig's voice softened. "Thorkell, you wiped your wife's tears away because you love her. Though her tears have long ago dried, those hands are stained with love for her, and what you need to know is this: the bitter events that are looming over you like a bird of prey can be checked. Stop letting your fear of the unknown cloud your judgment and listen to my words. I am no fraud; you have to trust me."

Thorkell looked down at his hand and then back at Rannveig.

"What do you want of me? What could a herder of sheep do for you?"

"You can kill the troll, Hragrun."

Thorkell was certain he had misheard the witch.

"I can kill who?"

"You can kill the troll, Hragrun, who lives in a cave on the Skagastrond. There is something in the troll's horde that I need. I only need one thing; one object- you can keep whatever other treasures you find there for yourself."

Thorkell laughed finally. His fear evaporated. He began to feel anger building up inside him. He knew of Hragrun; everyone in Langidal knew about the troll that made the Skagastrond uninhabitable. He was a monster of immense size, cunning, and viciousness. Though many had attempted to kill him, all had failed to a terrible price. Farm after farm lost their cattle and sheep to Hragrun, and the only thing the people could do was move further away from the thing's lair. Even boats wouldn't sail near the Skagastrond.

"You tell me you can help me, then you slap me in the face with an impossible price to pay for your help? I can't do what you ask. No man can."

"The troll is a beast that breathes and eats. It bleeds, and it can die," Rannveig said.

"A beast that stands taller than three men and has limbs thicker than trees!" Thorkell responded. "Mightier warriors than me have gone to kill it with many companions, and they failed. The thing is too powerful."

"They failed because the beast is not fated to fall at the hands of many, just one."

"Why don't you use your sorcery to kill it if it's so important to you?"

"The beast isn't fated to die by sorcery, either. One man will kill it."

"Are you saying that you've seen my future, and I'm fated to be that one man?"

"No, I'm not saying that. I can't see your fate that way; the spirit of your family-line is too strong; she stops me from seeing your doom."

"That's convenient for you, witch! What makes you think-"

Rannveig interrupted him. "Thorkell, I've asked many men to kill the troll. Some wouldn't do it because they feared me. Others wouldn't because they feared the troll. But you will do it because you fear something more than me or the troll. You fear losing your family more than anything."

Thorkell had to sit down. He pulled his axe out of his belt-loop, dropped it, and sat heavily next to it.

"I'm right, aren't I?" Rannveig asked.

"I feel like I'm caught between two ice floes," Thorkell said.

"You are in a way," Rannveig answered. "Come sunrise, you don't want to board that ship because you know the outcome of that. You don't want to go to the troll's lair because you're certain you'll die there. But I think you'd rather die than live to see the ruin of your family and the deaths of your sons. At least if you go to the troll's cave, there's a chance you'll see your sons live to be men."

"A woman who can see men's futures is now talking to me of chance," Thorkell said darkly. "I don't know how to take that."

Rannveig just smiled a bit at him.

"What's so important in that thing's stinking cave that you're willing to get others to die for it?" Thorkell asked.

"An arm-ring," Rannveig answered. "An ancient treasure crafted by hands on this island long before our people ever came here."

Thorkell furrowed his brow. "There were... people here before we settled this rock?"

"Not people as we know them. They were an older race, and they excelled in sorcerous metalcraft. They lived in caves that are still undiscovered, deep in this land."

Thorkell just stared at her. "Why have we seen no traces of them?"

Rannveig seemed impatient. "Their fate was done here, and they vanished away long ago. But their spirits are still here; I sometimes see them. The people here butcher cattle for them and pour the blood on hillsides hoping to keep them satisfied. Three years ago, Thorhall Gamlason and his men found some of their artifacts in a cave. He had the arm-ring until the troll destroyed his farm. I know that the troll has it now."

"What's so special about this arm-ring?"

"It has great power. I require it. That's all you need to know."

Thorkell sighed and put his hands over his face leaning on his elbows.

"So now you want me to choose between shame and the loss of my family, or suicide in a troll's den looking for a magic ring made by spirits," Thorkell said.

"No, Thorkell, I think your choice is already made," Rannveig said. "You and I must leave tonight so that I can hide you from Hogni's sons. My home is hidden about three miles from here in a gully. The moon will be low soon. If we leave under the cover of darkness, no one will see us."

Thorkell spoke up. "This is no plan, woman. Even if you could hide me from Hogni's sons, there's no way for me to reach Skagastrond. No one with a ship will sail near it, and it's too far on foot. I'd be found before I got there."

Rannveig just smiled at him again.

"There is a ship that will take you. Your father's friend Solmund will be arriving here two days from now in his ship. He will take you."

Thorkell had reached the end of his patience. He stood up. "I've grown sick of you acting like you know everything. You don't know men as well as you think. You can't know where Solmund is, and he wouldn't agree to this. Sailing is his livelihood. You are all just wild moaning talking about elves and trolls and nonsense. I think you're manipulating me because you know my misfortune."

Rannveig acted as if she hadn't heard him. "Solmund left Hrafnkelsstadir over a week ago. He'll be arriving here tomorrow or the next day. He'll help you because your father saved his life- that story is well known. He owes your father, but cannot repay a dead man. He can only repay the son. Solmund will do what you ask no matter how mad he may think it."

"How can you know where Solmund is? How are you so sure?"

"Berabrak has told me."

"Who?"

"The spirit that tells me of things hidden."

"This is all madness," Thorkell spat and turned his head towards Garmund's farm. From this distance, the fires burning there seemed very inviting. Rannveig spoke from behind him.

"Madness, maybe, but madness conceals a pathway to power as the Lord of the Runes has shown. Was it madness for him to stab himself and hang bleeding for nine days from a tree, all to plunge into the deeps of Hel? Most would say so, but he won great power and wisdom. You can win a treasure of no less worth- the lives of your sons."

* * *

A little while later, Vestein was staring at Thorkell in disbelief.

"What did I say before you went out there? Madness doesn't begin to sum this up!"

Thorkell had walked back to the farmhouse and found Vestein standing outside with Svein, Garmund's brother.

"Svein here can tell you how the witch entrapped Garmund and his wife."

Thorkell looked at Svein. "Is that right?"

"Garmund's boy, Arinbjorn, took a fever three moons ago, and no one could help him," Svein said. "Rannveig came in from the heath with some plants, chewed them up, and spit them into a kettle of water. She cooked it and told Alfhild to give it to him. Two days later, Arinbjorn was up, running around and laughing."

"That's how she operates," Vestein interjected hastily. "She ingratiates herself to powerful people by helping their children, winning her the protection she needs to carry on with whatever other evil she's planning."

Thorkell didn't respond. He seemed distant. Finally, he spoke. "She saved Garmund's son?"

Svein nodded. "Yes, and I think she did the same for Thorgrim- his daughter, Thordis, took sick, and she was laid low. They were preparing for her funeral when Rannveig showed up and put some walrus bones under the girl's bed. She sang those songs of hers, and the girl recovered."

Vestein laughed. "She's probably causing the same fevers she pretends to cure!"

Thorkell gave a hard look at Vestein. "As a father, deeds speak louder to me than words- and louder than your paranoia. I don't see evil in saving people's children from the maws of a fever-death."

Vestein stepped forward with a serious look. "She's bewitched you, man. You don't see it, but it's clear to anyone else who looks. She's using your children against you, too!"

Thorkell lost his temper. "Good! Then the Gods protect me! I'm bewitched, and I'm going to leave with her and go back to her hut."

Vestein turned his face skyward and threw his hands up. Svein just looked on, the line of his lips very tight.

"Listen to me now, Vestein. If you're my friend, you'll do what I ask."

Vestein ran forward and grabbed Thorkell's coat. "You're throwing your life away for that witch! Don't do this! I'd rather see you die fighting at the door of your farm than to have you eaten by a gods-cursed troll in his shite-smelling cave!"

Svein stepped forward to part them. "Thorkell, Vestein's right. This is suicide. Hrein Hermundarson and his men tried to kill that thing last year. He took his best fighters, and Hrein was a legend himself. The troll's too tall for anyone to get a shot at its head or neck. All they did was nick up its legs and put some arrows into it. It killed all of them except one, and they were bad deaths. It crushed men inside their armor like pig bladders. It even killed and ate Hrein's hounds."

"Don't forget to tell him about Tosti's ships."

Svein continued. "The troll waded out into the water off the Skagastrond and tore up Tosti Olafson's ship when the tide took them too close. Tosti's other boat escaped but couldn't help Tosti or his men. Their bones are probably still out there on the strand."

Vestein looked into Thorkell's eyes. "Would you expose Solmund and his ship to that? He'll die out there with you."

"I've done nothing to this woman. Why are you convinced that she's out to weave evil for no reason?"

Vestein couldn't contain himself. "Thorkell! How many stories do you need to hear? Evil people don't need a reason to do evil! It's just what they do!"

Thorkell regained his composure. "Vestein, I hear you. But I have to do this, and as my friend, you have to do what I ask. You said you'd die to protect my family. Now I'm asking for a lesser boon."

Vestein stared at the ground and shook his head.

"You have to tell Herjolf to go without me in the morning. Thank him, and tell him that I no longer need a place on his boat. You have to stay here. Rannveig says that in a day or two, Solmund will arrive. Have him wait for me."

"Do you know what you're asking me to do? You're asking me to collude in the death of a friend."

"I'm asking you to do this for me and my sons. If I leave here tomorrow as you want me to, my sons will die. If I stay, I may die, but I'll die fighting and feast with the heroes in Valhalla. After that, my sons will have their chance to join me. If I succeed, I'll see my sons live long enough to grow beards and have their own families. So, this ends well for me however I go. It's fate, Vestein; it's a father's doom. I have to do this. As a father, I have to try."

With that, Thorkell gathered his belongings and walked to meet the witch who waited for him on the heath.

VI. Rannveig's Hut

Rannveig's hut was a brittle dome of turf and hides with a central fire-pit. Fetishes of bone and fur hung from the inner walls. Drying herbs hung from the low ceiling. The whole place had a smell like faintly decaying flesh and pungent herbs.

Thorkell and Rannveig made good time. She knew secret ways through the rocks, and the sky was not yet grey when they arrived. Thorkell looked around before he went inside her shelter, wary of Hogni's men, but they hadn't been followed.

Before the sun came up, Rannveig offered what advice she could give Thorkell for the task ahead.

The sound of her rune-sticks clattering onto her floor brought Thorkell back from a daydream about his wife and sons. Rannveig collapsed forward over the bent twigs which were all carved with rows of dark red runes.

"The Lord of secret knowledge speaks through the runes," she said. "He has something to tell you that will help you to kill the troll."

Thorkell leaned forward.

"The man who kills Hragrun will not be armored nor will he wear a helmet or hold a shield" She said while looking down.

Thorkell, unwilling to voice his disbelief, kept his thoughts grimly to himself. *Wonderful. The fool who goes after the troll by himself will also do it naked. That's a fitting end to this story.*

Rannveig continued. "The land and the waters themselves will show him the way to victory."

"That's all?" Thorkell asked.

"Odin's words are few on this matter, but he has said all you need to hear."

Thorkell fell back onto a pile of furs. This was probably the last night he would sleep in the middle-world of men, and he was spending it in a witch's hut surrounded by her magic and madness.

He sat up again unable to let his life go so easily. "Woman, you've already asked much of me. This is too much. It was already madness to chase your troll, now you're asking me to give up what protection I have!"

"I know you're afraid, Thorkell; there's no shame in that. But don't fight this. It runs counter to your instincts, but then wisdom often hides in places that the instincts of men tell them to avoid."

"That's lovely, but it's coming from the mouth of a woman who doesn't have to face a troll soon."

"I've faced death many times, Thorkell."

Arguing with her was impossible. There was no way he was going to go into the troll's cave without at least a shield to guard his life. He fell back again into his furs and fell asleep. He expected to dream that night, but no dreams came.

VII. Troll, Ice, and Blood

Solmund the Mariner, son of Eldrin, did arrive as the witch predicted. Though he was aghast at Thorkell's request, he swore to honor it so they sailed away from Langidal and into grey waters.

Solmund showed the depth of his friendship by taking his boat to the Skagastrond. He promised Thorkell he would remain for a day near the shore watching for him. Thorkell told him to leave if he hadn't returned in that time. Hragrun's cave was not far from the shore; this trial was to be decided early in the day.

As the ship cut through the mist towards the strand, no one on board dared speak louder than a whisper. Vestein had come but had been curiously quiet during the short voyage. As Thorkell was preparing to leave, Vestein came up to him.

"Imagine the tale they'll tell when you get back," he whispered. "Thorkell, the Sheep-Herder will become Thorkell, Trollkiller. That alone would be enough reason for the assemblies to revoke your outlawry."

Thorkell looked at him and smiled. "Thank you for your confidence. If I don't come back, tell Elsa and my sons everything. If I can see what's happening from Valhalla, I'll expect you to keep your word to protect them."

Vestein went quiet. He leaned closer to Thorkell and put his hand on his shoulder. "May strong Thor, the killer of monsters, go with you and give you victory."

Thorkell finished tying on his armor and slid his axe into his belt-loop. He put a small silver hammer on a leather cord around his neck, picked up his helmet and shield, and dropped into the water. The men on the ship watched him walk up the shore and disappear into the fog.

The rocky terrain of Skagastrond was desolate. The only sounds were wind and the crunching of his boots on the ground. As he walked through the mist, visions of his wife cooking fish and baking bread taunted him. He could see his sons running and playing in the field next to his sheep. He wanted to get lost in the visions, but he kept leaping to alertness every time he thought he heard a noise.

About a mile in, the land began to rise steeply, and Thorkell decided to walk around the ridge. As he walked, Rannveig's rune-cast was bothering him. What if Odin actually did give Rannveig a message? Maybe stripping off his armor would be the ultimate sign of trust in the Gods that would render him worthy of killing the troll and of living a life with his family. He dismissed those thoughts, but they kept returning.

The ground beneath his left boot suddenly gave out with a loud crack, and Thorkell pitched forward. He had wandered onto a frozen lake and nearly fallen through the ice. He laid flat on the ice and pulled his wet boot out of the hole. He sat up and looked around at the small lake. He looked down at his boot and then over at his shield which he had dropped to free himself.

All at once, a smile spread across his face. Here on a frozen lake and amid his despair, Thorkell finally understood what the Allfather told him. He knew what he had to do and for the first time, a feeling of exciting possibility flared in his chest. "Okay, witch," he laughed under his breath, "Let's do it your way."

Thorkell stripped off his mail shirt and dropped it on the edge of the frozen lake. He dropped his helmet and laid his shield down. Holding his axe, he looked up at the ridge looming over the lake and started climbing to the cave-mouth that was visible a ways up.

Feeling apprehensive and lightheaded from the hard climb, Thorkell stood in the maw of Hragrun's cave straining to see into the darkness. The cave-mouth was strewn with the bones of cows and other beasts, and there was a stench of rotting flesh pouring from it.

Thorkell steeled himself and walked ten paces in before stopping, tightening his grip on his axe, and shouting "TROLL!" at the top of his lungs.

The echo of his voice in the cave was sharp, and it fell quiet after a few seconds. His eyes darted from shadow to shadow, alert to any sign of movement. From behind him, there was a slight crunching noise causing Thorkell to spin around in alarm. There, standing behind him at the cave's mouth, was a nightmare.

Hragrun, the troll, towering some twelve feet tall, his massive, heavy jaw hanging open to expose a row of yellow teeth, was glaring at Thorkell from the cave's entrance. The thing had been outside! Thorkell's eyes widened, and his heart began to race. Hragrun let out a terrible, thundering roar and raised its hands above its head.

Thorkell couldn't get by the troll so he ran deeper into its cave. He could hear the massive bulk of the thing plunging towards him from behind, and he could no longer see in the darkness. He expected to run into a cave wall or trip over a stone and be crushed by his monstrous pursuer.

With a shout, Thorkell hurled himself to the side hard against the tunnel wall. Hragrun plunged right by him before halting and turning, roaring in frustration. Before Thorkell could get back to his feet, Hragrun's huge, crust-packed nails raked across his chest and left shoulder, hurling him backwards and into a pile of bones and refuse. Thorkell pulled his axe against his body, rolled and kept rolling, his torso stinging like it was on fire. He could feel the cave-floor shaking under Hragrun's weight.

Leaping to his feet, Thorkell darted as fast as he could towards the cave entrance. Hragrun was still behind him howling in rage. Thorkell burst forth back into the dim light of day and immediately lost his footing and began to slide and roll down the side of the ridge. He let his axe go and it sailed down below him landing with a clink. Hragrun looked down at him, roared again in rage, and began climbing down with great swiftness.

At the bottom of the ridge, Thorkell snatched up his axe and began to run for all he was worth. His feet plunged into frost and puddles as adrenaline drove him to move as fast as he ever had. It wasn't long before he heard the beast behind easily gaining on him.

"Hragrun the troll, towering some twelve feet tall, his massive, heavy jaw hanging open to expose a row of yellow teeth, was glaring at Thorkell from the cave's entrance."

Ahead through the mist, Thorkell could see the frozen lake. He darted out onto the thick ice near the bank and headed onto the thin ice of the lake-center, his lungs burning. He could feel the frozen surface under his feet shake as Hragrun's feet landed on the ice to follow him.

Giving a final shout, Thorkell dove forward and slid across the ice gritting his teeth. If he had been wearing his armor, he wouldn't have made it that far; he would have fallen through the ice ten paces before.

Directly behind him, Hragrun let out a roar of shock as the lake's ice near the center split and broke underneath him. The massive bulk of the monster disappeared into the lake with a tremendous splash that sent ice-chunks sailing and caused cracks to cobweb the ice under Thorkell.

Thorkell turned and slid to the hole made by the troll's plunge and waited. He didn't have long to wait; Hragrun's feet could reach the lake-bottom, and the troll's snarling head broke the surface of the water as it struggled to free itself.

That was Thorkell's moment. With a loud cry and a wide swing of his axe, he sent the blade deep into the neck of the troll which was now at hip-level. The blade sank in but did not sever the head of the beast; a clean decapitation was prevented by one stubborn patch of flesh and tendons on the side of the thick neck. Still, blood spurted out of the gaping wound, and the monster's mouth went wide.

Thorkell pulled his axe free and swung again with all his might. Hragrun's head flew off and landed on the ice with a solid thud. Bright red blood spurted and ran from the twitching body which now bobbed in the water; it was hot blood which hissed on the ice. Thorkell, his face spattered with the troll's blood, screamed a loud shout of triumph; all of his adrenaline rising to a fever pitch of euphoria.

The victorious Thorkell staggered forward and buried his hands in Hragrun's neck-stump, bathing his hands in blood. "See here, Thor!" he shouted to the sky. "Old redbeard, killer of giants, look here! I am Thorkell, Son of Olvir, and I give the bloody remains of this foe to you!"

"Hragrun's head flew off and landed on the ice with a solid thud. Bright red blood spurted and ran from the twitching body..."

He ran both of his hands across his forehead, blessing himself with the blood sacrifice to Thor and shook the rest of the blood onto the ice around him.

* * *

A few hours later, Thorkell emerged from the troll's cave, holding a bag thick with gold and silver cups, rings, and other treasures. In his left hand, he held what Rannveig was looking for- the strangest arm-ring he had ever seen set with red gems. As he began to walk back to the shore, he noticed that the mist had faded. He closed his eyes and let the sun warm his face as he went.

The witch was going to get her magical arm-ring, the people of that coast were going to get their lands back, but Thorkell, Son of Olvir, was going to get the best prize of all: together, he and his wife would watch their sons grow into men.

***

'TWAS THE NIGHT BEFORE

* * *

The curve of the fork at the end of the knotty pole was perfect. The moonlight made every long groove in the wood fill with ink-black shadow. That same pale light made the world glow blue and illuminated every ice crystal swirling in the wind. From a low hill south of the sleeping village, Andro looked down upon the many snow-covered rooftops, let his eyes feast upon the golden, comforting lights shining from each distant window, and finally lifted his gaze to the north to take in the vast and dark forested ridge that wrapped itself around all of these works of man.

Andro ate the food of Elphyne and drank its wine. He put the pole between his knees and said the words. At first, nothing happened; all that he could see were white droplets in the blue air, and all that he could hear was the deep moan of the sky. But then the first spirit reached its hand up, cold and unseen, and seized him below the left knee. The spasm it caused spread up his leg, and the urgent restlessness began to seize all of his lower regions. And then, just like that, the great wind came with a silent rush and pulled him away from the ground.

Up he went, as though his body had no weight. The wind now ruled him as though he were a fleck of ice or a thin brown leaf. To and fro he swirled in the air as a beam of warmth shot up his spine and opened like a blossom in his brain. Then the wind blew harder and he shot in a straight line over the village.

One thick-snowed roof and then another, faster and faster, they went by. One pin-point of golden light, then another, and then just the dark ground- the old stone wall and trees choked in icy mist. Here, he knew he must go higher and higher he went. The ground sloped up; the ancient ridge climbed darkly. Up he shot, the village now a black blur in the blue snow far behind, and the trees racing a hundred feet below his toes. The crest of the ridge came; the sky was more intensely blue, and the vast landscape beyond was very black.

All but for one place- in the midst of the rolling hills and tangled forests, wolf and owl-haunted and dreaded by humans on nights such as these, a pinpoint of reddish-gold light stood out. None in the village could see it for the ridge, but stories were told of it. Neither the ridge nor the night were its real concealers; none but those who had eaten the food of Elphyne could see it. And now, Andro's flying-pole turned towards it without his needing to urge it so, and he streaked towards the very core of its glow.

Closer and closer it seemed to come as he flew without a sound through the ice and dark. The dead flew fast, and to eat the food of the Underworld was to be dead, for a time.

Now the light was large and dancing and twisting- a great bonfire atop a lonely hill. Andro circled the hill and slowly sank, sank again, and settled down. His bare feet gently touched the hard moss and smooth rock near the fire. He took his riding-pole in his left hand and walked with the lightest foot-falls to the far side of the hill, and then down the slope to the place where an ancient cave mouth yawned open to the world.

A hint of warmth and the echo of strange sounds emanated from the cave, breaking the snowy silence of the thick forest that surrounded the hill on all sides. Something below the hill made it seem to radiate a subtle heat, and yet the thin layer of snow forming noticed it not. A great clutch of desire suddenly gripped Andro's chest and stomach for he wanted to go inside, he wanted to go below. His steps became rapid, but the approach to the cave was still steady and slow. Nothing rushed into it; one only came to it as the dead must come.

And into its dark mouth he went. The ground immediately sloped downward with hard-packed earth, and once again in the great dark, a distant light could be seen. And with every step Andro took on the nighted incline, the distant light became brighter and a cacophony of sounds became more and more distinct. It was music but not like any music of the mortal world.

The dark slope finished, and a second portal was before Andro through which dazzling light poured- a light not bright but which filled his eyes with a luminous, stark glare nonetheless. Countless shapes and bodies filed past the door, and the drone of what might have been drums, pipes, and strings sang alongside the light. The only other sound was laughter though some of the laughs could not have come from human throats.

Andro stepped within the chamber of revelries. And there he stood, one man amid thousands of men, women, and other inhuman creatures who swirled together in dances or stood around long, stone-rimmed fires or dark wood tables drinking and eating. The drone of the music was interlaced with the drone of voices.

In the dark nooks of the cavernous walls, naked forms of men and women- or the coupled shapes of human and non-human entities- twisted hard together in loud passion. Some had not sought the cracks in the walls; some lay on the floor around the chamber's massive central fire heavy in rut with one another. The other dancers and carousers watched them with satisfaction or lascivious glee while others took not much notice of them.

The tables were long and countless; the fires were many. Over some of the fires turned roasting-spits; throughout the gathering doe-faced women dressed in green silk slid and floated, handing out silver cups to any who asked. Andro saw men with the heads of deer; heads crowned high with forked antlers, and men with the heads of goats; some were bedecked in multicolored finery while others went naked and hairy; their cloven feet clopping along the cavern stone. Half wolf, half-human beings snapped and snarled as they tore into meat from the tables or chewed at it on the floor. There was no way to tell what humans here were alive or dead- for all were dead and all were alive. It made no difference.

"Now the light was large, and dancing and twisting- a great bonfire atop a lonely hill."

Andro looked high above the revelers and saw Them sitting on a great stone platform high above: He sat to the left in a great throne carved of wood and bone; his great antlers spreading; his handsome, dark face tilted towards his Queen whispering something in her ear. He was fully naked, and the great phallus that hung snake-like between his legs was on display for all to see and admire.

But nothing would match his Queen's beauty; she was draped in a flowing white gown with strange pearl-like stones arranged in intricate patterns all about it, and her long, dark hair fell around her with a hundred tiny ornaments and braids. Her face was as pale as marble- the face of every woman that had ever died, and her eyes were as black as the void of space. Her throne was gleaming black stone from the heart of the world.

Andro glided through the crowd and came to stand with his riding pole before their great high seats. They both turned to gaze on him, but he did not meet their gaze; he took a knee and bowed his head. He didn't need to look at them to lock his eyes with theirs; his soul's eyes never looked away from them. His body merely showed homage to the Great Ones. He knew words would not suffice to express his reverence so he tried no words; he let his soul illuminate itself with all the love and respect he was capable of. And like a firefly, his soul added to the ghostly light of the cavern of the dead. In the lands above, this same emotion illuminated nothing the mortal eye could see; here below, it was the only light there was.

The Old Ones smiled even though their faces moved not. "Andro Man" their lightning-like words slid into him; "We accept your tithe of reverence and recognize you as our man. What can we give you, alongside the hospitality of our hall?"

"He sat to the left, in a great throne carved of wood and bone, his great antlers spreading, his handsome, dark face tilted towards his Queen, whispering something in her ear."

"I come from a sleeping world of cold and despair, kindly hosts. Grant me the boon of remembering what it is like to bend a knee in your presence, for in the warmth of that memory, the chill of the forest will be as fresh as May to me."

"Granted, Andro Man" the Queen said. "Lift up your face, now." Andro slowly looked up and was grasped by the blackness of her eyes- a black beauty that made him feel like dying on that spot and remaining here forever. The Queen's face became icy and her lips parted only a bit before freezing cold air suddenly pushed its way into Andro's mouth and filled his chest. What was put inside him grew warm and turned small circles behind his heart.

"Give that to the next mortal men and women you see", the Queen said. Then she sank back further into her throne and became like a star in the night.

Andro stood up, floating now in a different way, and turned to the revelers and worshipers who still tilted and darted and mingled behind him. A brown-haired woman that he recognized from a village just to the south of his own pushed through the crowd with two reddish glass cups. They only smiled at one another; he took her cup, and her invitation to come to the feasting table nearest him.

Andro took a sip from the cup, felt the warm rush of ecstasy move down his body, and immediately back up to his face. All cares were banished, and his soul felt perfectly at peace. The spices used to mull this translucent gold wine did not grow in the human world. Gone was any trace of fear or pain or regret from his life above. Gone was his cynical desire to retreat from the world for all its evils and sorrows.

There was beauty there, and he knew it; the wine let him remember it. There was beauty everywhere. He looked over at the brown-haired lass and under the spell of the wine, her face had formed itself into a light brown hare's face. But her eyes were still so human, or something other-than-human or animal...

She re-assumed her human form now as lovely as the rose she was, and they cast their cups away and ran together to the central fire of the endless cavern. They spun around and around with endless energy and unquenchable joy. Their feet, it seemed, did not touch the ground. The music began to grow smoother and combine into harmonies that spoke of a spring that was everlasting. Andro no longer saw the crowds, the beast-shaped people, the pale dead, the Queen or her strapping Lord; he saw only the brown-haired girl and soft, warm light, spiraling upward towards the surface of the world.

* * *

An eternity later, Andro Man opened his eyes. He was as rested and warm as a man could be despite the cold overhead and all around. The white light of morning was everywhere; the sounds of a distant bell floated alongside the snort of a horse, and two men laughing at some bawdy joke. The scraping sound of a woman outside the wall of his hut clearing her throat and spitting something on the ground rang in his ears.

He closed his eyes again, and the memories came back, soft and beautiful. He had made love to the girl for what seemed forever. He had spoken to the bull-horned women that came from Glen Etive, and they had told him about the coming fire that would eat through the houses of his own village and claim six lives before the snows were gone. He remembered conversations about wars to come; wars that had long ago been fought; and the stories told by the dead of those wars.

He saw the ancient powers with bent bodies of watery, scaly flesh; the immortals who slumbered under the mountains. He heard their rages at their holy places being put under the axe, and their joys at strange powers forming together in deeper caverns below this one. What changes would those weird unions mean for the world, long after Andro's passing? He had no idea. He saw the local Laird's dead children wandering through the cavern, all three in perfect serenity now, a world apart from the misery of the fever and coughing sickness that took their lives. They told him what places he should never go lest he be caught and strangled and burned for his witchery.

Andro stood up, light on his feet still, feeling no cold. It was the day of Christ's birth, and all in the village began to walk towards the kirk to hear of the glory of the child who was born to conquer hell and banish death.

***

MEADOWSWEET'S RED CHAPLET

***

"It is an unfortunate fact that the bulk of humanity is too limited in its mental vision to weigh with patience and intelligence those isolated phenomena, seen and felt only by a psychologically sensitive few, which lie outside its common experience. Men of broader intellect know that there is no sharp distinction betwixt the real and the unreal; that all things appear as they do only by virtue of the delicate individual physical and mental media through which we are made conscious of them; but the prosaic materialism of the majority condemns as madness the flashes of supersight which penetrate the common veil of obvious empiricism."

-Howard Philips Lovecraft

The Witch House

***

I'd say that I arrived at the old house around six or so. It was the middle of summer, so there was still some daylight left. Getting into the place was certainly no problem as time had not been very kind to the windows or the roof of the house. I was able to let myself in with only a short hop onto a windowsill.

Now like anyone who lives near the town of Barrowfield will tell you, the old Towneley estate is quite a ways out of town, over in the Pendle Hill country-a never-ending collection of fields, abandoned farmland, brooding woods, and low hills. Perfect, if you ask me; the countryside was just as grim as the legends attached to this old house I was preparing to spend the night in.

I call it "perfect" because I needed all of the macabre ambiance I could squeeze into my desperate "let's find inspiration in the rotting middle of nowhere" project-and this old place had the look, the feel, and the history that practically wrote stories for you.

I am a writer by profession, if indeed writing can be called a profession. For me, up to this point in my life, it always seemed more like a masochistic kink: a matter of handing my heart out so that other people could flippantly tear it to pieces, after which I could go home dejected, looking forward to my diet of fifteen cent oriental noodles and water. I guess it was sheer pride that kept me trying-or some deeper, more vagrant urge that doesn't even have a name.

I had recently begun seeking inspiration from the past. Everyday life in the modern world was dull to me, and history was always my favorite subject. The countryside surrounding me was full of its own history; a less-known, secret history that only the locals were privy to. It was the kind of history that got passed over as local stories and superstition, but that had unlimited potential for the dreamer or the ambitious writer.

I was always something of an amateur folklorist, and I remember waking up one depressing evening three weeks back, after a long restless nap, to find myself flooded with the memories of stories I had heard as a young boy about the old Towneley estate and the doctor who had tried to live there with his family so many years ago.

To be fair, the countryside is packed full of every kind of ghost story, witch legend, and ghoulish occurrence that you can dream of. To the old folk, every hill and country cemetery, and every boarded-up, abandoned hospital with an overgrown graveyard behind it was a nightly witness to a parade of supernatural activity. I think that this shire had more haunted houses and woods than the rest of the country put together.

But the country around Pendle Hill was especially famous up here. To begin with, it was thought to be a meeting place for witches since time out of mind. It seems that in the late 1600's, a branch of the wealthy Towneley family built a very large manor out in that countryside on the edge of the woods west of Pendle Hill.

These Towneleys were an odd lot, to be sure: the matriarch of their family, Dame Sybil de Towneley, was legendary in her own time as the "great queen" of all witches in this shire. Stories about Old Dame Sybil were told to me by my own grandparents. They told how she was ageless, and how she rode from Pendle Hill to Boulsworth Hill on certain nights with her white familiar-cat *Pelling Jill* perched in the crook of her black-draped arm. She rode to meet her lover, a great and wicked huntsman who lived in the Boulsworth woods, and whose ghost was sometimes spotted or heard in the night often around the same time that a camper or a hiker went missing out there.

The Towneleys built their house in lonely seclusion, and as the stories went, held great feasts and orgies to their master, or their "king" who was never quite identified in any source. But he appears in the local folklore regarding the northern country as the *King in Secret*. Of course, the church and the social authorities at the time considered this unknown king to be none other than the Devil himself, but that always struck me as the typical and unimaginative

conclusion that all of the country clergymen came to when presented with lore or customs of possibly ancient origin.

So the Towneley family held their legendary witches' Sabbaths in seclusion, and were supposedly often joined in their feasts by their master himself and by the "hidden folk" who lived out in the woods and in the caves under Pendle Hill. This went on for quite a long time before the family seemed to die out; the local history simply stops mentioning them after a point, except for the stories of the ageless Dame Sibyl still riding about the Countryside.

"They told how she was ageless, and how she rode from Pendle Hill to Boulsworth Hill on certain nights with her white familiar-cat Pelling Jill perched in the crook of her black-draped arm."

All of this makes for quite a good campfire-story, which brings us to the well-known rumor surrounding the next family that restored and moved into the old Towneley manor around 1860: a country doctor named Edward Thorne, alongside his wife and his young daughter.

On this point the local legends say even less: only that the doctor, his wife, and their entire staff disappeared, leaving just the little girl alone at the house... a little girl who was found later totally oblivious of her parents' disappearance and innocently playing with a tea-kettle full of what seemed to be blood. I know it sounds strange, but that was how the story went.

Quite predictably, dark rumors circulated and got darker as time passed. The house was abandoned and never lived in again.

So I decided to change that; to write a new chapter of the legend. Scary legends of witches and disappearing people are always interesting; it's almost faddish in the big cities to play "witch" and be interested in the occult and in paranormal phenomenon. I find that most people have at least a passing interest in these subjects, no matter what. So I resolved to go spend the night up at the old Towneley House, and see if I could be inspired to write a story about what might have happened there.

I didn't really know what to do or to expect; I suppose I had all kinds of fantasies of finding some clue as to what really happened to the Thornes or of just seeing or hearing strange things. Either way, I wasn't afraid to try. I was born fifty kilometers from Pendle Hill; I grew up in its shadow; I wasn't afraid of my own countryside, or any of its legends. If anything, I figured that Dame Sibyl might be amused for a change to have someone unafraid to approach her and to ask her how things were in her neck of the woods. I felt that if the Thornes were now unhappy shades wandering around in their house, they'd be happy to finally have a biographer reveal their true story to the world.

Many people, including my few friends, would have given me a hard time about my idea, or worse, decided to sneak out to the old house on the night I spent there for the purpose of playing pranks. So I kept my plans to myself.

This whole plan had one more dimension of which you should be aware. As a struggling artist of the written word, I sometimes indulged my senses in hallucinogenic substances-all for the very noble purpose of heightened creativity, of course. If you've ever ingested hallucinogens before, you already know that where you do them is very important. Every place has a different "feel" to it; every place inspires different visions when your altered mind-state experiences it. The happy, silly trips you had around friends at a club were totally different from the ones you had in the dark, peaceful park at night when you were alone.

My drug of choice was the golden-sprinkled mushroom that grew in the fields past the Apps farm out on Lockley lane. For my special night, I had brought seven good-sized caps with me, courtesy of my good friend Ian. I told him that I'd be giving them to a friend in Leeds who wanted to try them. A small lie, but I wanted no complications.

I just wanted to get out to the house, get inside, look around, wait for the sun to start to go down, swallow my mushrooms and spend the next nine or ten hours having visions of macabre, gothic beauty and mystery.

Looking back, I guess what I really wanted was for the old folklore to live again; I wanted to see faces in the ground, hear witches chanting out in the night around red fires, and see the little folk of the Pendle Hill woods. I wanted to see ghosts, hear the Dame's horse go by, hear screams, and try to understand (as only a tripping man can) how a place can become *more* than just a place with the passage of time: how it can collect the drama of human lives lived out within its walls, and accumulate so many curious folktales until it becomes a new realm all its own.

* * *

I am pleased to report that there were no complications; I parked my car at an abandoned house outside of Clitheroe, somewhere down Pendle road. I walked east and crossed A59 and headed into the fields. Pendle Hill was massive all across the horizon in the nearby distance. It didn't take long to find the remains of the house, based on maps I had seen.

As I said before, time had not been kind to the old place, so getting in was no chore. I was very impressed by the dust covered, bare-board remains in the house; there was no real furniture to speak of, but there were empty shelves and mantles.

On one of the mantles there was a lump under the dust which turned out to be a small picture frame with a faded last-century photograph of a very young girl holding a basket of flowers. I didn't want to make any guesses; I wanted to get under the influence of my fungal muse as soon as I could, because I was a little disturbed once I got to the creepy old place and realized that the sun was rapidly fading, and that I would be there alone in the dark soon whether I liked it or not. At least while I was tripping I would have no sense of the slow passing of time. I could just swallow the mushrooms, have a flight of imagination, and before I knew it, it would be morning.

Well, that was the theory, anyway. I sat down in the large front room of the house, with leaves and dust all over the floor, before the remains of a very large fireplace, and I swallowed my caps. I waited in the shadows there with the twilight outside, listening to a scraping noise in the ceiling above me which soon became the sound of an owl hooting at the darkening sky. In those parts, twilight was called the *owl light*, and I was always happy to make connections.

I zoned out for a while before I started to feel strange. My legs began to tingle, which told me that the alkaloids in the mushrooms were beginning their work. I stood up and felt slightly dazed; it was very dark, but I could make out the immense shapes of the rooms around me. I stumbled into the adjoining room, the one with the old picture on the mantle, and felt very ill. I emptied my stomach out in the corner but could not see the mess I had made, as it was so very dark. I realized that there was no pain, either; my senses were numb and I felt lightheaded.

I walked softly back into the room with the missing window that I had let myself in through and then walked right back out and towards the distant sound of laughter that I heard coming from near the fireplace. It sounded like a little girl. I went into that room, and sat down as a thousand waves of multi-colored, invisible light began to sweep through my head. I started to snicker uncontrollably at the idea of a little ghost girl running around this really creepy old house.

I felt like there were rainbows in my hands, and the trees outside had taken on a strange luminescence. It filled this large room with light, a light that was so bright it allowed me to see my shadow. After a long, profound moment of mental silence, my shadow detached from me and slithered away.

***

Pelling Jill

I walked in peace, as though in a dream, to the front door and opened it. I knew that I had been sleeping for a long time, and that I had to move around some now. I looked outside and was filled with a great sense of peace and satisfaction by what I saw.

In the field before the house, in the strange day-like glow, there was a young girl skipping along and picking flowers. She was dressed like the girl in the old photograph, only this little girl was real. She was grinning and enjoying the simple pleasures of life as only a child can. I'd say she must have been about five or six years old.

I strolled down the front steps to the house and felt the soft grass under my bare feet; how my shoes got off I will never know. I enjoyed the feel of the grass; it was like a thousand warm, writhing currents of air under my feet. I smelled the sweet scent of the pollen in the air and walked up behind the little girl, whose back was to me, her bonnet totally obscuring her face.

Right as I got near to touching her, she turned around and glared at me. Instead of the little blond cherub that had just been laughing and picking flowers, there was an obscene, scaly and dark face in the bonnet. It had yellowish, glowering eyes that were full of all of the animalistic malice of nature, but tinged with a devious intelligence that was ages older. Its mouth was cracked open, exposing a row of teeth that were like a shark's; I almost had to vomit again with the fear that shot through me like a bolt of electricity.

"After a long, profound moment of mental silence, my shadow detached from me and slithered away."

I fell straight backwards onto the ground, shocked, as the monstrosity leered at me for about three or four more frozen seconds. Then it faded away into a cloud of little darting insects. The sweet smell of the pollen was gone. It was night again, and I was sitting alone outside the Towneley house with my head spinning.

I began to panic a little; some part of my mind still seemed to remember that I had swallowed a handful of hallucinogenic mushrooms, and I started to become paranoid that maybe I had poisoned myself. Perhaps, my imagination reasoned, I had gotten the legendary "black mushroom" in my handful and was now dying. I started to have trouble breathing and to feel a sense of impending doom. My anxiety attack ended suddenly when I heard something behind me.

I heard a soft padding noise and turned to look at the front porch of the house. There, a white cat was slowly walking down the steps. I didn't seem to mind this; I thought it was kind of funny actually, and I snickered to myself as this white cat walked straight towards me.

The approach of the cat was suddenly the last thing on my mind, for right then I heard the sound of a horse screaming out in the fields before me. I jumped to my very numb feet and could feel my guts shaking as the unseen horses pounded the ground. I was terrified that they were going to run over the little girl, so I ran out into the dark field waving my hands and yelling.

I don't know how long I did this before I remembered that the little girl was actually some kind of green scaly horror, and I gradually stopped caring whether or not a horse trampled her to death.

"Instead of the little blond cherub that had just been laughing and picking flowers, there was an obscene, scaly and dark face in the bonnet."

Around the same time, I stopped caring, the loud sounds and the vibrations also stopped. To my wonder, I could see people riding on horses through the fields, silently toward the house. They were dark figures, and they rode along with my eyes tracking them. When I noticed the house again, it was all lit up with lights shining from all its windows, and looking in much better repair than it was before.

I looked down at my feet and noticed a white cat cleaning one of its rear paws. It stopped when it felt my eyes on its back and looked up at me with round, dark feline orbs. We locked eyes for a moment.

I said "Hi" to it.

It said "You are in danger here" to me, right back.

Around this point in time, I remember laughing at this as though it were the funniest thing that ever could have happened to me, or anyone else, at any time. Granted, a cat speaking *is* funny, but in a very terrible, reality-shaking kind of way. Not a comical one.

But I laughed so hard that I cried, and when I cried, I really started crying. I think that something in me realized that this was a bad dream that I couldn't wake up from. I started to feel a sense of dread that I could not shake, and I wanted to walk to my car and go home. I didn't want to see scaly little girls or talking cats anymore. I didn't want rainbows in my hands or horses running silently around. I thought maybe I'd go write about dog shows over in Liston or fictional harsh reality period pieces about the Boer war.

I looked down at the cat again, and it was still staring. My world had become a pastel darkness, a great whirlpool of coldness and moonlight and screeching insects. I began to shiver, standing out in the cold field in front of this old house, and talking to a cat.

"I looked down at the cat again, and it was still staring.

The cat said "Come on and walk; the Master will be coming soon."

It walked away from me, off to the east, and I followed it even though I couldn't feel my feet very much.

I asked the cat "So where is the little girl?"

It replied "Dead and gone, friend, for many years now. What you saw was no descendant of Adam and Eve, but the old Bergamot who was called to this place centuries ago by the Grand Array of my mistress."

I was listening with much interest to this talk, when I suddenly found myself staring at the grass and becoming mesmerized by the undulating motion it was making in the moonlight. It was like a thousand serpents with rainbows playing about their mouths, offering warmth and understanding to me. I stooped down and grinned, trying to remember this sight, and wondering why everyone I knew took things so seriously. I could feel that everyone I associated with had a dangerous problem with stress; that they all took things far too harshly. There was no need for all that.

My reverie was interrupted by the white cat, which now had a glaring look in its eye. "Reject this absent-mindedness of yours, and you may yet live to see another dawn" it said. "Not that it matters to me, truly. What happens to you now is up to the Master."

"...I suddenly found myself staring at the grass and becoming mesmerized by the undulating motion it was making in the moonlight."

I had some interest here. "Who is the Master?" I asked. "And where are we going?"

The cat said "Only the Vanishing People can tell you who the Master is. It is not my place. I am not great enough to speak his name."

So we continued walking east. I felt like a door was opening up in my head. I started to feel very warm and to imagine that I was seeing a portal of seven layers, stretching from my head into the heavens themselves. All things in the universe felt beautiful and still. The cat next to me trotted on, and I found myself walking onto what looked like a long and narrow track.

***

The Vanishing People

***

I was walking down this track running east from the old house, where hundreds of moths were fluttering all about. There were strange rocks standing everywhere. The remains of old fires were just black lumps by the greatest of the stones, and the wind was suddenly warm. It was nighttime, and yet I could see as though it were day.

I was dressed strangely; not as I had been, but I thought nothing of it. I didn't recognize the strange shoes that I was wearing, nor did I remember getting shoes back on my feet.

There was a river or a long narrow weir up ahead of me, and a dark ribbon of forest far across the water. It was calling for me to come to it with happy haste. I wiped a bead of sweat away and started to move faster. I forgot all about my strange feline companion.

Right at that moment, a hare ran across the track with a fox in hot pursuit. Halfway across the track, the fox stopped short, turned its head in my direction, and flicked its white-tipped tail.

It regarded me for a few seconds, and without a sound, it became a young man. He was bronze-faced and he carried a twig of what looked like birch wood. He smiled and said "I shall tell you the song of the Master, the King of this track, who comes in every dawn." He then sang in a strange, high-pitched voice:

"A gentleman who carries Light, white and gold;
The tree-shadows lengthen; His glory is grand!
The Lord of the array, with gold and brass,
With plates and bells, and horns a-marvel;
Keeper of the ways in hidden rows, the horses' tracks,
His gathering resounds and echoes joyful;
His star rises and shines, His hooves are hard,
And radiant His tines, His head of fire."

And with that, the man faded away into one of the strange stones. I heard the white cat say to me from a distance "Come now into the light of the trees."

So I wandered off the track and into the woods, and I could hear the white cat's voice from somewhere far away telling me "Near at hand, the three sisters made their home."

I felt impressed, as though I wanted to meet these three sisters. But I was more in awe at this wood: majestic and living and so sweet of scent. These strange trees concealed mysteries older than man. It was the *forest primeval* that you only read about in the works of the Romantics. I felt like I was in another world.

I passed near a clearing where a two-tined forked pole stood upright from the ground with the remains of a fire smoldering before it. I could see visions in my head of shrouded people convening there in secret. A few moments later, I came to a hidden road striking through the woods; a narrow track that the white cat told me was called "Robin's Road" and which I guessed was aligned to Pendle Hill further south.

I heard a buzzing somewhere near, and saw a bee-hive dripping with amber honey. One of the bees buzzed closed by me, and in a moment it had become a young woman with golden hair and a dress the color of straw.

She looked at me for a long moment and she said "I shall tell you the song of the King of these woods, these trees which cradle the south-winding track." She sang, in a voice as smooth as silk:

"Dark Satyr with foliage about the crown,
Hobgoblin and Master of the wooded hall-
He lays His head in living boughs!
The birds scream His name: seed that saves!
And the woody silence is thick with glee,
Impish Lord of the fields' own life;
May dancing rings, red days and red nights,
In the woods before the hill."

And with that, the honeybee-woman faded away leaving me with the hum of the bees and a slight feeling of faintness in my heart.

I had to lie down and rest; I was feeling numb all over. I was brought back to awareness by the white cat pawing at my face and kneading me with its claws. Without understanding why, I stood up and started walking back to the Witch-house.

I turned and walked back to the crumbling edifice in the midst of it all; the dark windows and gray wood of the house stood out on the edge of the hill-wood as a second twilight seemed to overtake the spectral world. An Owl called hauntingly from that unseen nest in the fragile roof. A darkening moor spread out to the west of me, and I walked quietly into it along a track that cut across it like a pale ribbon. This track was called the "Ghost Road" by the white cat.

All the while I could hear the Owl calling far behind me. I fancied I could hear the sounds of the unseen dead muttering to themselves their final regrets; I looked for their shapes in the dusk, but I was more frightened not to see them there. I imagined them jealous of my life, trying to drag me with them across the river of time.

I heard a deep croaking and I saw a great toad staring at me from the soft, dark ground. It moved once, its muscles sliding under its bumpy skin, and then it became a thin, white haired man.

He looked through me with his empty eyes and said "I can tell you the song of the Master of the water's edge, whose blade runs red with the blood of all the dead of the world, coloring the sunset itself crimson."

"Right at that moment, a hare ran across the track with a fox in hot pursuit."

He sang, in a raspy tone:

**"In further places, a distance from the narrow way,
Past where the Elder stands, and a stable bare for hay,
Black ground and red sunset there,**

**Where the mare of the Queen may wade
For forty nights and forty days, there
The river red and dark drains wide:
The Old Man of the Lady's word, fierce bright,
Will ferry the mournful dead to weer reside;
And all will bow before the Lass."**

And with that, the toad-man faded into the newborn night. I could no longer see at all.

Scared and alone, I did not want to see the river that this ghost-road led onwards to; I walked back to where I knew the old house was and veered out further into the country with the cold wind from the north stinging my face. The moon would not rise for a long time in this new night, but the first faint stars were there to keep me company.

I pressed out further north along the faint track that ran into the unknown, with the night countryside watching me from all sides. This was the kind of night where the entire world watched a person. And this road, I knew, could lead down as far as Hell itself.

I had gone so far that I didn't know where I was anymore. I fancied I heard dogs howling and yelping in the distance, and perhaps the sound of a horse crashing through the bracken, when suddenly an Owl swooped silently by me, startling me. It landed on the skeleton of a dead tree nearby and folded its wings, staring at me with its unblinking gaze.

I stared right back, but it was gone. Under the tree there stood a luminescent woman with hair and eyes that were very black. With no moon and a few stars, I could see her plainly: she walked forward and told me "I know the song of the true King, the *Faery King* who sometimes rides this way on nights such as these. I shall tell you, little man."

She sang, in a cold voice:

"There, dead from life, the other place,
Dark and continuous, my hidden land;
Dark to living men, and dark the King
That sweeps in with winter's wind-
The Lord of invisible places, the Son of Art,
Black cloak and mount, and cold of heart,
Words in dark wood and draped in black;
Wise and furious, Wind and wiser still."

And with that, she too was gone; although I thought I heard an owl call from far away. I sat down and began crying my eyes out, and for the first time I realized I was freezing cold all over. I think I must have fallen asleep out there because I have a big blank spot in my memories around this time. I may have wandered around jabbering to fence-posts or to dead trees. Countless strange mental adventures are possible in every hour of these fungus-dreams, but I have no way of knowing what I did. I just don't remember.

***

The Master's Book of Poems

***

Later, I found myself sitting on the front steps of the old house. The moon was high, bathing the countryside in pastel and white. I felt perfectly euphoric as though nothing was wrong in the entire world. The white cat was there with me, cleaning itself again.

My eyes scanned around the glimmering nighttime countryside and I could see a strange, dark figure, very short, standing out in the field near a tree line staring at me. It cracked a smile and the moonlight glinted off its row of teeth. Even from such a distance I knew that it was the terrible thing that I had mistaken for the little girl.

I felt alarmed. I had to ask the cat "Is that thing going to come over here? Are we safe here?"

The cat glanced over and said "Who can say? He is very hungry all the time, and he has not had a proper meal since the last people who came here."

I swallowed hard and started to feel my chest tightening up. I finally made a decision.

"I'm going inside" I announced, and stood up as the world tilted to an odd angle. When it righted itself, I walked up to the door and stopped short.

The door was solid and new, with a huge rack of antlers spreading from a mounting above it. The windows were all shuttered and the large front porch was clean. A very old-style broom leaned to the left of the door. The house had been resurrected. It was no longer a ruin. I could hear commotion inside: people talking and laughing and I could see a glow from under the door.

I tried the door, but it wouldn't open. I glanced up at the strange decorations, and then back over at the cat which was standing and staring at me.

Before I could ask, the cat said "Why don't you ask them?"

It nodded its head to the left. I looked, and I saw a dark line of people, both men and women, walking towards the front of the house. They were dressed in very old-style clothing, looking like peasants and gentry from three centuries ago.

As they approached the house it seemed as though a spotlight fell upon them, lighting up their pale, sweaty faces and their stringy hair. They all seemed to be intoxicated, bordering on hysterical, and the lead man had a long pole with what looked like bull's horns mounted on it. Some of the women were carrying poles carved like phalluses, and others had brooms which they waved in the air. They all stopped before the front steps of the house, facing the door, and began chanting in a loud, single voice:

**"There are horns above the table,
And horns above the door!
Three horseshoes in their place,
And hard planks for the floor!
The hearth is dark, and wind the voice
In the house of the family of the old faith!"**

They wouldn't stop chanting this; they bellowed it over and over. Some of the women screamed it; one woman fainted, sending some of the others into laughing fits. These people didn't seem to notice me and I watched them with wonder for a few minutes.

Then I turned around, and, suddenly gripped by a strange hysteria, started screaming the words of their song. I didn't know it by heart; I just yelled the words that I did remember. I started dancing around the porch, stumbling over the words and my own feet, and doing my best to ignore the white cat who had started laughing at my antics.

The porch went quiet and the door swung open. The revelers were gone; it was dark again, and I was alone. I could see the cat's white tail disappearing beyond the door. I followed it in and closed the door behind me.

It seemed to me like I was stepping into a 1930's black-and-white movie. The air inside this room even had what appeared to be film grain static. I looked around and the room *flickered* and became "colorized" again. It became still and rich in dark browns and reds and long shadows.

The great room was eerily alive; time seemed to have reversed itself and old furnishings had re-appeared, as well as dark-framed paintings. The house was full of activity; I could hear people laughing and talking distantly through the walls.

The front room was still dark. The fireplace was not lit, but the mantle was covered with beeswax candles and lamps burning low, still casting a soft glow onto my face and the large painting above the hearth.

The painting was spectacular; it was of three horsemen in nighttime forest scene. They were all darkly clothed, and the rider in the center had a bow with an arrow nocked, the string drawn back, and a rich golden aura radiating about his head. The man to the left of him had a long golden staff with two serpents circling around it, and the man to his right had a bright lantern in his hand. These three figures had shadow-obscured faces, and the full moon was visible in the painting's dark blue sky. A brass plaque on the lower part of the frame, under the painting, said:

MENS ILLUMINAT

I stared at the Latin plaque and at the painting for a while, dreaming in my head that the trees in the painted background were moving. The voices in the house started to sound closer; they seemed to be in the long room beyond this one, the old dining room that I had climbed into originally. It sounded as though they were singing and stomping their feet or hitting their hands on a hard surface rhythmically.

I walked towards the sound of the noise, which sounded very much like a party; I heard a deep-voiced man cry out:

*"In the name of Orvendale the doors are opened!
In Hyldor's name the doors are closed!
In our Master's name the lamps of art shed light!
In our Lady's name the wainscot is sealed,
And the grounds are kept aright!"*

To this, the throng of voices all cried out:

*"Below the horns and round the table,
We await the light from the east!
We raise our cups for the archer's luck,
And the Master of the feast!"*

I had my head against the door into the dining room, listening to all this. At that moment I pushed the door wide open. As it strained on its hinges, the noises within all ceased.

The dining room was empty of people. There was a very long oak table there with many chairs, and a great set of horns on the wall above the large chair at the far end. There were candles all along the table and burning dimly, giving the room an aura of sable and gold. There was an-other fireplace on the far wall with a smoldering flame in it.

In the chair below the horns there was a man sitting, looking at me. I was rather impressed by him- so impressed that

I suddenly felt very sober. No euphoria, no dizziness, no absent-mindedness. I was feeling very solemn and together. The man's eyes never left me.

"There was another fire-place on the far wall with a smoldering flame in it."

He was tall, as best I could tell considering he was slouched in the chair, but he had long dark hair and a thin, neat goatee. He had a light complexion and a narrow, elegant nose. He had a baggy white shirt on with open laces. He smirked a bit and leaned his head to the side, waiting to see what I was going to do.

I should interject at this point that I am (as far as I know) straight. I've never been attracted to a man before, but this man was quite different. He had a beauty about him, an almost feminine beauty. I found myself feeling oddly attracted to him. For the first time since I came to this house and made the mistake of dropping mushrooms into my stomach, I also felt a real sense of trepidation, as if there was a chance that I might not be going back to my car or my life after tonight.

found a bit of courage and decided to make the best of it. I walked up to the side of the table and asked "Mind if I sit down?"

The man smiled and said "Be my guest."

So I sat. He leaned forward and rested his arms on the table, and I noticed that he had a thick leather-bound book next to him. He watched me. It was an uncomfortable silence, so I broke it.

"So where is everyone?" I asked. "Sounds to me like they were having a good time in here."

The Man said "They are all here. They belong to me. I've bade them go upstairs while we talk."

"So, you must be the man himself, the 'master of the feast' as they call you. Is this the case? Are you the guy in charge here?"

"If you wish to put it like that, yes," he said. "But I find that undue attention paid to such titles keeps a distance between people. I'm just someone that wishes to help those who are lost to find their way."

I thought I understood that. "So who are you really?" I asked. "I mean, I think I'm a little lost, as far as understanding what I've been seeing tonight."

"I am just the one who came here to help. Some of your kind have found me to be of great service and thanked me with feasts and praise. They have also chosen to stay here with me till time is no more. I oblige them, allowing for their feasts and their revels to continue for all time. When a person understands what I have to tell them, their lives are replaced by unending joy."

I didn't quite know what to make of this man. I asked "So where did you come from?"

"From a quite a distant place, but at the same time, not so far away, to the mind that understands."

I was now getting a little annoyed at what I perceived as evasion on his part. I grinned a little, and threw out the next thing that came to my mind. "Did you come from heaven or from hell?" I asked, not sure that I even believed in such things.

"Not from one place or the other" he said. "I move back and forth between them."

I glanced outside the windows of the dining room but all I could see was darkness. I felt like this room was somehow separate from the house itself, floating in a great void.

I looked over at my host and said "Look, I just came here to stay a little while. I wanted to write a story about this place, just make up some stuff that would get noticed, make me known locally, you know? I didn't know that you lived here, or that people were still here, none of that. Far as I knew, this place has been abandoned for a long time."

He spoke up at that point. "There are reasons why you thought as you did. In your mind, all you can see is an abandoned house. But try to understand that your mortal mind only sees a small portion of what is actually around you. Have you ever wondered where the past goes? Whence does the river of time flow? Where are the lost of this world to be found? My people have all come to under-stand this most sublime of truths: that "reality" is much greater than anyone thinks, or can think. When my light comes from the east, it illuminates the fullness of existence. Anything is possible to those that comprehend. If you had the choice, what would you choose to experience? Where would you choose to remain?"

I didn't know how to answer. "I would choose to be back in my life, writing. I suppose if I could be successful doing that, I would be happy."

"And what would you write about?"

"I'd write about the strange dreams that I've had here, and that I must still be having. I'd write about the Thorne family. I'd make up some something to explain their disappearance."

"Do you think that you are dreaming?" he asked.

"I don't know" I said. "I better be. I hope I am. Maybe it's the mushrooms."

"In the chair below the horns there was a man sitting, looking at me."

He leaned back in his chair and shook his head. "No, it isn't the fungus that you ate. You see me now and you see this house as it was because I allow you to. You are not dreaming. You are simply seeing in a different way."

"Why?"

"Better that you ask a bird why it flies south in the winter, or a bud why it breaks into blossom. My will springs from a mysterious source; I offer no explanations for it and I need none. Count yourself lucky that I have received you."

"So am I awake or asleep?"

He blinked once and said "watch."

He waved his hand and suddenly, the room went dark. I could see myself sitting on the dark and dusty floor alone, talking out loud to the decrepit walls.

Then the dining room returned and I was "me" again.

"What you just saw is what you call 'real.' If another were to wander into this house right now, they would see things as you just saw them. They would think you a madman for talking to the walls."

I started to feel disoriented again. "You have the power to change the world?" I asked.

"No, I have the power to change how your mind experiences the world."

"Can you stop me from dying?"

"Yes, but not in the way that you think. Death is another worldly event that surrounds you every day. I can change how you experience it, but nothing can stop it from coming to pass. You are mortal, and it is your fated lot."

"But what about all the people here?" I interjected. "If they are 'having a feast until time ends', then they must not be dying!"

"They have passed through the change that you call 'death' long ago" he said. "But they had a very different encounter with death compared to the person who has not received my light. As far as my people are concerned, their deaths were as the parting of a curtain and a horse ride back to this house, where I sit at the head of this table forever, filling their cups with sweet drink and bringing the light of an eternal dawn."

"What is death like for others... for those who don't belong to you?" I asked.

The Master leaned forward, looked deep into my eyes, and just smiled. There was something sinister in the smile and in his apparent refusal to answer.

I looked over and I noticed the white cat lying contended on the far end of the table, opposite the Master.

I said "Hey! It's that cat!"

"Yes" he said. "You have met Pelling Jill. She guided you in my name away from danger."

"Pelling Jill! I've heard the stories! That was the great Dame Sibyl's familiar spirit!" I was pleased with myself, to seem like I knew what I was talking about to the Master.

"Yes" he said. "I gave Jill to Sibyl."

"So you have always been here at this house? Ever since it was built?"

"I've been out and about since long before your kind realized how to build even the crudest of shelters. But the answer to your question is yes, I have been here since Dame Towneley and her kin built this house."

"So you know what happened to the Thorne family?"

"I do."

"If you told me, would I be able to leave here and tell others?" I asked. "Or does knowing what happened mean that I can't leave?"

He looked at me for a long moment and said "I can tell you what you want to know."

His hand came to rest on the large book in front of him. "It is all recorded here. Do you want to hear the story of Meadowsweet?"

I wasn't pleased with his answer, but I shook my head 'yes' anyway.

"You may not wish to know after you hear it" he said. "But then, wisdom is a child of experience, and usually of the harsh variety. So please, feel free to ask me any questions you may have as I read."

"What book is that?" I asked as he picked it up.

"A book of poems that I peruse from time to time. They amuse me."

He cracked it open. He flipped several pages and scanned silently for a moment.

"Ah, here it is!" he said. "One of my favorite poems: it is entitled "Meadowsweet's Red Chaplet."

He began:

"Meadowsweet's mother is no more,
And her father's gone too;
Gone the maids and the gardeners,
The servers and hands,
Once so many in sunlit days,
Now dwindled to few;
Who keeps the house from webs and dust?
Someone must.
And yet there is no one there.
And so it lies in disrepair,
Though Meadowsweet doesn't care.

Meadowsweet's name is Bethany Thorne,
The only daughter born
To Doctor Thorne and a pale young wife.
Picking lily-white flowers
In the fields and woods forlorn
This was Meadowsweet's lonely, happy life."

"Bethany!" I thought out loud. "That's right! The little girl's name was Bethany!"

I had remembered only because I had a distant cousin named Bethany. It was hard to believe that I had forgotten in the first place.

The Master was watching me. I felt embarrassed. "Oh, sorry. Please, continue."

So he read on in his smooth, perfect speaking voice:

"A sweet young girl of Adam's race,
With a rosy, lovely face;
Filling her bonnet with white flowers
In bloom one day-
Dressed in a child's dress,
With pink bows and lace.
But who knows what sleeps in the garden bottom
And the wood?
Curious folklore so often hints and warns
Of the spirits in trees, and fields,
and houses and barns.
Meadowsweet met a friend,

A secret friend, in the hedge-
With a red, toothy grin
And scaly skin green:
Bergamot the Red Faery,
Hungry that day, made her pledge
To tell no one of what she had seen."

"Okay, stop right there." I said. "Pelling Jill told me about Bergamot. I've become quite a student of that particular grinning nightmare. He was outside a little while ago. Who or what is he? Is he a *faery*? What's a faery? I've heard all the stupid stories, but call me silly: I think you're the man to ask about the hidden reality of those stories. Am I wrong? And... right before you answer me, you should know, Jill has already said that Bergamot was 'called here by the grand array of her mistress.' So, best I can figure is that Bergamot was something summoned here by the coven of witches that originally used this house. Am I right?"

He nodded and narrowed his eyes. "Yes, you are."

"And this coven called itself the "Grand Array" and Dame Sibyl was its earthly leader, and you were the "Master" that they worshipped, right?"

"Yes."

"How did they come to know you? Did you just introduce yourself to them? Is there a way of getting in contact with you in some old book somewhere or something like that?"

He smiled. "You were a lot more likely to meet me walking the roads of this country back in those days. Things were different then. There were more people back then that knew me from stories that their own families told them or stories that had been passed down for a very long time. And yes, there are some old books that mention a few quaint methods of getting my attention, but those are mostly quite outdated by this point. The easiest way of arranging a meeting with me is simply to come to my house. Which you have done."

"This is the only place you can be found now? In the backwoods of Lancashire?"

He said "Once again, remember that for your mind, this place may seem like a ruin near a hill in the shire countryside. But for me, this place touches every other in many hidden ways. All a person needs is to be lost, have a desire to find their way, and their wandering hearts can lead them to my door no matter where they are."

"So you are everywhere?"

"After a manner of speaking, yes."

"Now what about Bergamot? And the faeries?"

"Bergamot is another son of mine; I have so many. But he always took after his mother more than me. And the Faeries are another kinship of beings, like your people but still different. They share your world, but you do not see them because your minds do not comprehend their spaces."

"But Bergamot is a little monster. A reptile. I've seen him. The poem described him. I got the idea that he wanted to eat me. How is it that he is your son? Is he a faery or not?"

"I told you, I have many children. Bergamot is among the less developed of my children. He only thinks with his lust for flesh. And if he is remembered in the folklore of your kind as a *faery*, it is only because, more often than not, when the country people encounter the unknown, they always ascribe the activity to faeries. I have such tales of faeries to share with you, and these tales are not always as bright and lighthearted as modern tastes would have them. There was a time not so long ago when men and women better knew the true nature of the shadowy thickets beyond the fields of sight. They knew that some of the hid-den folk were a danger, always hungry for flesh, or for more delicate things."

"Why was Bergamot summoned here by the Grand Array?"

"You'd have to ask them."

I sat back in my chair, wondering what else was all over the world that mankind couldn't see or fathom. "Are you going to read the poem some more?"

"Certainly" he smiled. He continued:

"Meadowsweet, precious child,
Delight you in the white petals?"
Asked Bergamot. "Oh yes sir, I
Love them a lot!" said she;

"Like you also red roses, and
Sweet tea in the kettle?"
Asked he. "More than anything,
Sir I love them so!"
"Then say no more" replied he,
"And soon by the dark moon,
I shall satisfy you and me."

Meadowsweet's secret was kept,
And every day she would play
A grand tea party, with roses
And her secret friend.
And the moon shrunk steadily,
When at night she lay
And slept, dreaming of tea and roses
In the springtime wind.

Mr. Smythe the stableman
Was the first to disappear.
"Bring a friend to walk with you,
Meadowsweet dear"
Bergamot bade her- "Everyday,
Bring someone to the woods here
Then run away and make them play
A little hide-and-seek.
I shall surprise them and trick them
Merrily with my power-
And in return I'll give to you
A blood red flower!"

I cringed inside a bit. Pelling Jill had stood up now at the end of the table, almost as though excited by the poem. Her feline mouth was cracked in what looked like a smile. Her teeth also seemed darker than I last remembered them being.

The poem continued:

*"Ms. Valerian was the next
To take an afternoon walk
With the laughing innocent Meadowsweet,
Such a treat;
The woods were a magical place
To hear the child talk-
Where the lily-white blossoms
And red petals meet.*

*Soon there was no cook, no gardener,
And then no maid;
They left their employer without notice
Or so it was thought-
Mayhap they disliked seclusion,
Or were not getting paid
Enough from the coffers of good Doctor Thorne.
The house grew silent,
But Meadowsweet filled a toy-chest
Full of lovely red flowers that she loved best."*

I started to feel quite ill again. Pelling Jill yowled in pleasure. The Master raised his eyes to me.

"Are you well? You don't look it."

"I'm fine. I guess I just realized how, I don't' know, how really insane this all is. I'm not taking mushrooms ever again. I feel like dying or waking up from all this."

"It gets better just ahead" The Master said.

"I just bet it does" I said, hoping that I wasn't wearing out my welcome by smarting off to this majestic being who might well have been the devil or perhaps a god.

He continued:

"Finally, the moon was dark,
And that day Meadowsweet came
Out to play with Bergamot the
Red-grinning sprite;
"It's time to take mother out to play
In our little game" said he:
"She may enjoy a playful little fright."

"But mother is always in bed"
Meadowsweet said
"And father says she must rest
For I've a brother in her belly!
She must not move, to save strength
For the birthing ahead."
Bergamot's smile could not have
Been broader. "Then I shall go to her
And play my tricks within the house,
Meadowsweet: as the sun goes down,

Let me in, and the game will be complete."
"Mother and Father will tonight
Play hide and seek, and then you
Can make a chaplet of the red flowers I gave!
I shall give you three more
And a kettle of tea- just don't peek!
For if any see me play my tricks,
They must go to a grave!"

About this point I did begin to regret asking about what became of the Thorne family. I don't think the old rumors ever said that Mrs. Thorne was pregnant. That was a new and lurid detail that I thought I could add when I wrote all this down, if I ever did. I had mixed feelings. And I wasn't feeling any better, physically.

Pelling Jill's tail flicked in excitement and her eyes had grown big and black.

The Master read:

"The dark night settled, and Meadowsweet stirred.
In silence she went downstairs to open
The great double-door.
Such sweet thoughts filled her head
Of roses and violets;
As she hid her face in the parlor
chairs, Bergamot went upstairs
And the shrieks of fright and
delight were soon everywhere!

How lovely is childhood-a time truly free of cares.

Meadowsweet's friend was gone,
Never to be seen again.
She found his final gift:
Three sticky red flowers and a kettle.
She added these to her chaplet
Of red blossoms and then,
Wearing her pretty crown, set the
Kettle to boil and settle.

Mother and Father Thorne, and their unborn,
Were gone.
Meadowsweet worried for a minute
Then turned her mind to tea:
A thick red tea, sweet with sugar
and rosemary from the lawn.
How Meadowsweet loved the tea,
More like a jelly, though.
The next day came, and she laughed,
And played by her-self;
Wondering where her friend had gone,
That friendly red elf."

Right about that point I let it go on the floor next to the table. I didn't think that there was anything in my stomach after my first little retching, which seemed like ages ago. But apparently there was. I coughed and straightened myself up.

I looked around and saw that the Master had his book closed. He was staring at me with a sardonic grin on his face. Pelling Jill walked right towards me, put her face in mine, and when her mouth opened, black fluid leaked out.

She screeched, in a foamy, gurgling voice: *"Toadstool cursed dream! Toadstool cursed dream!"*

And the Master started laughing. I tried to stand up in panic, but I felt frozen; and right then, the world receded from me and I knew peaceful blackness.

* * *

I woke up, and it was daytime. It was dull outside, overcast and dreary. There was a little drizzle. I was lying in the dust of the abandoned back room of the Towneley house, where I had let myself in the day before. I tried to lift my head, but my hair stuck to the floor and I had to painfully yank it loose. My hair had gotten stuck in what looked like a dried vomit puddle. I stood up and felt very clear in my head. I walked into the front room, slowly, trying not to make any noise. I looked on the mantle for the old picture of Bethany Thorne. I found it and put it in my pocket.

I went out of the same window that I came in and walked away from the old house without looking back. I liked the way the drizzle felt on my face. I made it to my car and went home. It was good to be home.

I lay on my bed for a long time, just thinking. I don't think I'll ever go out to that countryside again.

But deep down inside, a part of me longs to return.

***

ABOUT THE AUTHOR

Robin Artisson lives in the *Green Meadow* of rural New England, sometimes on Maine's stony and forested shores, sometimes jaunting through the wooded interior, but always enjoying that region's four perfect seasons, its old and strange spirits, and its kindly and quiet people. He writes, conducts seminars devoted to spiritual ecology and sorcery, and is presently at work creating the *DeSavyok Elfhame Tarot* with artist Larry Phillips.

Printed in the USA
CPSIA information can be obtained
at www.ICGtesting.com
CBHW031650290724
12369CB00036B/694